DARJEELING AND A DEADLY DISAPPEARANCE

A WATERWHEEL CAFE MYSTERY

VICTORIA TAIT

A Kanga Press Publication © 2023

Cover Design by Daniela Colleo of StunningBookCovers.com
Editing Allie Douglas

For more information visit VictoriaTait.com

PROLOGUE

Dear Reader,

I felt compelled to tell this story.

We, as human beings, don't have to twist a knife or fire a gun to cause someone's death. And sometimes, not taking a stance, or turning away and ignoring a situation, is just as bad as being mean, nasty, or even cruel.

As the Cotswold's Rural Enforcement Officer, I'm an advocate for community policing: a collaboration between the police and local residents. Many cases would not be solved without valuable information provided by members of the public.

But some people use the ill fortune and distress of others to further their own fame and notoriety, particularly on social media. Such individuals are not regulated, but are quick to criticise us, the police, for any mistakes we make, or guidelines we misinterpret as we endeavour to solve complex cases and provide answers and closure for those affected.

This story is testament to all hardworking police officers who strive, amid criticism, and often far worse on social media, to do their jobs, uphold law and order, and ensure justice is served.

I hope you enjoy Darjeeling and A Deadly Disappearance.

Keya

CHAPTER ONE

A raindrop hung from Sergeant Keya Varma's black peaked cap and dropped to the soggy ground. Rain in the Cotswolds in June. She hoped it cleared up before her sister, Zivah's, wedding in just under two weeks' time.

"We'll finish the roof today and complete the second electrical fix and plastering inside by the end of the week," the site foreman, Vic Peters, said, removing his yellow hard hat and scratching his head. He seemed oblivious to the rain.

They were staring at a single-storey brick extension to a three-storey, nineteenth century flour mill, built of honey-coloured Cotswold stone.

The flour mill had been converted into Akemans antiques centre, but Vic and his team had almost completed renovating the rear ground floor area into Keya's new Waterwheel Cafe, complete with its own waterwheel. Or at least Keya hoped that would be the case and that the waterwheel would be refurbished and reinstalled in time for the opening.

"And I asked around the office, and one of the directors suggested we speak to a new company about the fit-out. It's run by a local boy who's been learning his trade with a large shopfitting outfit. I've organised to meet him on site tomorrow at 6pm, after he's finished work on his current project in Cirencester. Is that OK with you?"

Keya smiled gratefully. As a police officer, the Cotswolds' part-time Rural Engagement Officer, she had no idea about construction, and fitting out, whatever that meant.

But despite the rain, her chest felt light, and she smiled in pleasure. She was excited about opening a delicatessen in the brick extension, as she wanted local people, and visitors to Akemans auction house and antique centre, to try high quality local products at affordable prices.

Her eyes sparkling, she turned to Vic and said, "Thank you. I really do appreciate your help. And I'll see if Gilly can attend. She's far more creative than me and understands shop layouts and that sort of thing."

Gilly Wimsey ran the antiques centre and a small pop-up cafe at the monthly auctions. It was Gilly's idea for Akemans to have its own cafe, especially for the busy summer months, and Keya had persuaded her that she should be the one to run it.

But Keya's enthusiasm gave way to a flutter in her tummy. Could she really run a cafe? What about the staff, and ordering ingredients, and the cooking ...?

"Shall we join the others?" asked Vic, breaking into her racing thoughts.

Keya took a deep breath and followed him across some recently laid flagstones which would be the cafe's outdoor seating area.

They descended some steps to the River Coln. Gilly Wimsey, Gilly's father, Marmaduke Carey, and her aunt, known to everyone as Aunt Beanie, were standing on the riverbank, staring at an empty stone channel. It ran along the back of the mill, separating it from the swollen river water.

"Thank you for agreeing to pay for repairs to the waterwheel channel, Dad," Gilly said.

"Nonsense," interjected Aunt Beanie. "It's good business practice. When you own an old building on a riverbank, you need to pay for its upkeep. People underestimate the power of water, and the devastation it can cause."

"Well, I know Keya is delighted, aren't you?" Gilly said as Keya and Vic joined the group. Without waiting for a reply, Gilly continued, "And so am I. It's fantastic to think of customers sitting in the new cafe watching the waterwheel turn as they sip Darjeeling tea and nibble on homemade biscuits."

Gilly smiled brightly despite the rain, her mass of unruly orange curls hidden beneath a wide-brimmed waterproof hat. Keya was grateful to her, not just for the opportunity to run the café, but because she always had a kind or encouraging word.

Marmaduke Carey grunted as he tugged up the lapels of his tweed jacket, which matched his flat cap. He turned to Vic and said, "As everything appears under control, I'll return to the auction house."

As Marmaduke left, Aunt Beanie exclaimed, "This is so exciting. I can't wait to see the waterwheel in action. When will that be?"

"Rowan reckons his team's ahead of schedule, and they'll install it at the beginning of next week," Vic replied.

Rowan Cartwright specialised in restoring wooden buildings, vehicles, and heritage pieces.

"Fabulous!" Aunt Beanie declared.

Keya loved Aunt Beanie's eccentricities and exuberance. But today she was wearing a sensible, long wax waterproof jacket. Instead of her usual brightly coloured headscarf, tied in a large knot at a jaunty angle on top of her head, she had a plain brown one wrapped around her head to protect it from the rain.

"And no more dead bodies," remarked Aunt Beanie.

"Don't tempt fate," replied Gilly, her voice shaking. Gilly had known the two people whose skeletons had been found during refurbishment work on the cafe.

Investigating their deaths had consumed most of Keya's time in May, and after she and her colleagues at Cirencester Police Station had caught the killer, she'd had to catch up with her Rural Enforcement Officer jobs. But the upside was plenty of time off in lieu over the next few weeks to prepare for the cafe opening and help her sister with her wedding.

Keya's initial trepidation about the wedding had turned to eager anticipation since she'd tried on the amazing outfit Zivah had chosen for her. And her sister's wedding dress was stunning. She was looking forward to an amazing day, and already felt prepared to rebuff those aunts and other relatives who chastised her for not having a husband.

"Keya," called Gilly.

"Yes?" Keya pulled herself away from her thoughts.

"Vic said he's organised a meeting tomorrow with the shopfitter. I'll try to make it, but it depends if Peter can look after the kids." Gilly's husband, Dr Peter, ran his surgery out of part of their house in the neighbouring village of Coln Akeman, and his patients covered a wide area of the rural Cotswolds.

"I'm sure I'll be OK if you can't," said Keya, knowing her voice sounded squeaky. She wasn't at all certain she would be able to cope.

"I'll come, and bring Norman with me, and we can grab a drink at the pub afterwards," Aunt Beanie suggested.

Norman Climpson worked part-time at Akemans as a porter and he lodged with Aunt Beanie, helping round the house, and with the animals on the farm where they lived.

Aunt Beanie grinned. "And you can tell us all about the ghost which is upsetting the villagers of Coln Akeman."

CHAPTER TWO

The rain continued through the night and when Keya woke the following morning, she heard it spattering against her bedroom window.

Downstairs in the small kitchen of her semi-detached house, having showered and dressed, she boiled the kettle and contemplated a variety of teas on the shelf above it.

She was trying out different teas and checking their taste against the notes she'd been given at an afternoon tea cookery course earlier in the year.

She usually drank coffee in the morning, especially before work, but she also enjoyed a cup of refreshing tea in the afternoon.

Today she decided to try Darjeeling again. A black tea from the Darjeeling and Kalimpong region of India. Her notes told her this was important as it was the only tea protected by a Geographical Indication trademark.

She sat down with her china cup and saucer, decorated with yellow and red roses, and a matching teapot. She'd bought them both, and five other cups and saucers, for only £10 at Akemans antiques centre, and they were ideal for her tea-tasting sessions.

Continuing to read her notes, she remembered that tea aficionados considered Darjeeling the finest tea in the world and that adding milk was a sacrilege as it ruined its delicate flavour. OK, she'd try it without milk.

She poured tea into her cup and sipped it. Did she taste citrus fruits and flowers? She wasn't sure, but the bronze-coloured liquid was sweeter than Earl Grey and she thought she could discern a fruity aroma. It was pleasant, but she still preferred it with milk.

She added a splash, pushed her tea notes to one side and pulled a blue cardboard folder towards her. Since it was raining, and she didn't have the excuse of going out, she decided finally to try and work out how she wanted to set up her deli.

Luckily Gilly was in charge of fitting out, and more importantly, paying for the cafe. She'd drawn up a licence for Keya's use of the premises, and reading through that was another task on Keya's to-do list.

She unfolded a large plan, which Vic had provided, and several smaller, photocopied sheets of the single-storey extension. It consisted of a small room for Keya's office and a larger open-plan space for the deli. But what was she going to sell?

She'd been so busy with her police work that she was way behind researching and speaking to local suppliers. Which meant that anything she put in the deli now, like shelves and tables, would need to be portable so she could change the layout as she added more products to her range.

She started searching online for examples of other delis and found Pinterest, which was a gold mine of images. She found some amazing delis selling a huge array of items, but most of them were large barn-like spaces.

She only had a small room, so she had to keep it simple. She definitely needed a counter to stand behind so she, or whoever worked in the deli, could serve customers.

Examining the plan, she saw that Vic had pencilled in a serving area beside the wall which separated the deli from her office, and he'd left plumbing for a wash-hand basin. But should the counter be glass-fronted and refrigerated?

If she wanted to sell local cheeses or meats, they would need to be kept chilled. And what about freezers for frozen items? There was so much to consider. It was exciting, but daunting.

Her phone rang.

"Hello," she said hesitantly. The caller was Ryan, PC Jenkins, her friend and colleague from Cirencester Police Station. But was he calling for social or work reasons?

"Morning, Keya. I didn't wake you, did I?" asked Ryan, a note of concern in his voice.

"No," she smiled. "I'm looking through examples of other delis, trying to decide what to do with mine. There's so much to think about."

"What are you selling?"

"That's the trouble. I haven't had time to research and meet suppliers."

"Then why don't you leave it for the moment and concentrate on the cafe? You could always sell a few sample products there and see what customers like. There's no point rushing into it and losing money."

She hadn't thought of that, but Ryan was right. And she didn't have money to burn. Just her limited, hard-earned savings.

"That's a brilliant idea. Why didn't I think of it?" Keya enthused, but she also felt a wave of relief and a lightness in her chest.

"Because you have so much to think about and you've been busy working. Which is why I wondered if you wanted a break, and to meet up with Ozzie and me tonight? It's been over a month since we had a meal together at your local pub."

"I have a site meeting at six," Keya remembered, "and then Aunt Beanie suggested drinks at The Axeman in Coln Akeman."

"Perfect. Why don't Ozzie and I meet you there, say seven thirty? We can all have a drink, and food for those who want it." Ryan was a tall, young man in his mid-twenties who also kept himself fit. He didn't like missing meals.

"OK." Then Keya steeled herself to ask, "Any interesting cases?"

"Not much. The gossip is all about that ghost of a woman that has suddenly materialised in Coln Akeman. It's a good job you're on leave, as Inspector Evans has been rebuffing calls to hand the case over to you."

Inspector Evans was Keya and Ryan's boss. He was a grumpy

Welshman, but Keya knew his heart was in the right place and he was loyal to, and protective of, his team.

"Why me?" she asked.

"Because nobody else wants it and they consider it a rural offence."

"How can a ghost be a rural offence?" Keya rolled her eyes. But in a way she did understand. As a female Indian police officer, she'd been handed cases nobody else wanted her entire career.

"Anyway, as long as no harm is done," continued Ryan, "the Chief Constable has ruled it out as a police matter. But maybe we can catch a glimpse of the ghost tonight and hear what the locals have to say."

"Ryan!" Keya scalded. "You shouldn't encourage them." She could almost feel his boyish grin on the other end of the phone. "I'll see you later."

Smiling indulgently, she finished the call, but as soon as she placed her phone on the table, it rang again. Zivah's number.

"Hi, sis. How's it going?"

"Oh, Keya, you won't believe what's happened!"

CHAPTER THREE

"Calm down, Zivah," said Keya into her phone as she poured herself another cup of Darjeeling tea. "And tell me what the matter is." She sat back on her wooden kitchen chair.

"I have to cancel the wedding."

"What?!" Keya sat up quickly, knocking the table. Tea sloshed from her cup. "Oh toda!" she exclaimed grabbing the building plans. Luckily the saucer had caught most of the errant tea. "Why?" she asked, stuffing the plans for her deli back into their cardboard folder.

"Because the wedding venue is double booked," cried Zivah.

"But you organised that over six months ago."

"I know! But Mum, Dad and I are at Charbury Castle Hotel now, and the new events manager has just told us that the wedding booked on the 16th is in the name of 'Farmer', and they booked it over a year ago."

"Let's not panic, Zivah. I'm sure there's a simple explanation. Do you want me to come over and help sort it out?"

"No, Dad's been great and really calm and helpful, although I can't say the same for Mum. I had to take her outside when she started shouting at the hotel staff. Dad said 'Farmer' is the name of the groom and they're an influential local family who owns a chain of jewellers.

"The manager refused to give Dad their contact details, but he looked at the manager's notes, when she wasn't looking, and the bride is called Natasha Nkosi, or at least that's what he thought her surname was. And she lives in Coln Akeman. You know people there. Could you find her and ask her if she'll change her wedding to the Saturday? You know I can't move my date. The priest spent ages consulting the stars, and Friday 16th June is the perfect date for our ceremony."

"I don't know a Natasha Nkosi, but Gilly Wimsey might. I can give her a call. But do you really think she'll agree to move her wedding date? Would you?"

"Keya!"

"OK, OK. I'll find her and speak to her." Keya doubted the other bride would agree to move her wedding, but showing willing and trying to find her would at least calm Zivah down and give her space to think.

As long as she didn't spend the rest of the day with Mum, who'd either complain bitterly to Dad and demand he sort everything out, or call her friends and act out the drama again.

"And then do you want me to come over?" asked Keya.

"Just find this Natasha for me, sis."

"All right. I'll do that right now," Keya reassured her, before finishing the call.

She stood up and carried the teapot, cup, and saucer to the sink, tipping away the remaining tea. What she needed now was a coffee.

While she waited for the kettle to boil, she refolded the deli plans and, this time, placed them neatly back in their folder. Ryan was right. With her sister's upcoming wedding, and her police work, it was sensible to concentrate on opening the cafe for the moment. She'd have time to work on the deli later.

Sitting back down at the table with her mug of coffee, she called Gilly Wimsey.

"Morning Keya," answered Gilly. "The kids are going to Mum and Dad's for tea tonight, so I'll make the fit-out meeting."

"That's great, but it's not the reason I'm calling." Keya told her about her sister's call. "So I'm trying to find this Natasha Nkosi. Have you seen or heard of her?"

There was a pause at the other end of the line.

After several moments, Gilly responded, "An attractive young woman recently rented a cottage opposite the green. I saw her when the kids were playing French cricket with some friends. But I don't know what she's called, and I haven't seen her in the pub or the post office."

"And there's nobody else living in the village who could be her?"

"No, I don't think so. If she was a long-term resident, the WI ladies would be brimming with gossip about an imminent wedding. And I don't know of any other newcomers."

"Thanks, Gilly. Can you remember which cottage you saw the woman in?"

"Rose Cottage. It's the one with pink roses climbing up the wall."

Finishing the call, Keya considered her day. It was no longer the pleasant, relaxing experience she'd been relishing. She checked her watch. Half past ten.

By the time she'd driven to Coln Akeman and found the other bride, it would be lunchtime. And then she really ought to meet up with Zivah and check she was OK, and see if there was anything else she could do. Which meant she might not be home before her meeting with the fit-out contractor at six.

Keya spent the next twenty minutes making sandwiches for lunch. She'd already prepared an egg mayonnaise filling. She added a teaspoon of Dijon mustard to it and snipped some chives from a plant growing in a pot on her windowsill.

Deciding to make extra sandwiches, in case she met up with Zivah, she removed a bowl of homemade hummus from the fridge and spread it onto slices of seeded bread, adding thin slices of cucumber, and pieces of pickled vegetable for a tangy taste.

Packing the sandwiches into Tupperware containers, she placed them in a red spotty cool bag along with bottles of sparking water and elderflower presse, an assortment of crisps, and a bar of Dairy Milk chocolate.

Delighted that the rain had stopped, and patches of blue sky were visible from her kitchen window, she added an ice pack to keep everything cool.

Gathering up her bag, the blue folder, and the picnic, she grabbed her coat in case it rained again, and piled everything into her metallic reef-blue VW Polo, and drove to Coln Akeman.

Leaving her car parked beside the village green, Keya followed the footpath towards the River Coln. The first houses she passed were large, but they gave way to a row of two-storey stone cottages.

Their front facades were plain, unlike the much-photographed Arlington Row in Bibury, but each had a pretty front garden, and the honey-coloured stone had a warm, inviting feeling when the sun shone on it.

Rose Cottage, with pink roses climbing up a trellis to the left of the main door, was the second cottage along. Keya opened the metal front gate, walked up the flagstone path and took a deep breath before rapping on the door with the rose-shaped door knocker.

There was no reply, although she thought she heard a door close inside the cottage. She rapped again and waited. She was aware of movement in the window on the other side of the climbing rose and then the door opened, just a crack.

"Hello," said a woman's deep, rich voice, but it had a nervous tremor.

"I'm sorry to bother you, but I'm looking for Natasha Nkosi."

"Why? Who are you?" Keya could only see one clear blue eye, and part of a tanned face framed with long dark hair as the nervous occupant hid behind the door.

Keya hesitated. She wasn't on duty, and she didn't like to abuse her position as a police officer, but if she didn't gain this woman's trust, she wouldn't be able to help Zivah.

Removing her black wallet from her jeans pocket, she opened it up and showed the woman her warrant card. "I'm a police officer."

The door flew open. "What's happened? Is it Ezra? Has he had an accident?"

Switching into comforting police officer mode, Keya replied, "Please calm down. I'm not the bearer of bad news."

She halted, allowing her words to sink in. The young woman standing in front of her, who she gauged to be in her late twenties or early thirties, was striking. And tall. Her tanned olive skin accentuated her pale blue eyes.

Keya bet that if she smiled, she'd have perfect white teeth, but she wasn't smiling. Her face had changed from alarm to concern, and her blue eyes held a haunted look.

Instinctively, Keya asked, "Are you all right?"

The woman stepped back into the shadows. "Of course. Why shouldn't I be?"

"No reason," replied Keya apologetically. This meeting was not going well. She hadn't gained the woman's trust. Quite the opposite.

She decided to take the direct approach. "Are you Natasha Nkosi?"

In the dim light of the hall, Keya saw the woman nod.

"And are you getting married at Charbury Castle Hotel on Friday 16th June?"

Natasha's shoulders slumped. "I am."

Keya narrowed her eyes. That wasn't the response she expected from an excited bride-to-be. She ploughed on.

"My sister, Zivah, is also getting married that day. But there's been a mix-up at the hotel. A double booking. Would you be willing to move your wedding?"

"Move the wedding!" exclaimed Natasha. Then she stepped forward into a beam of sunlight falling on the open front door. She tilted her head to the sky and closed her eyes.

In a dreamy voice she said, "I'd love to move the wedding. Cancel it all together. Ezra and I have joked about flying away to get married on a remote Caribbean Island."

Natasha opened her eyes and looked down at Keya. Her voice still soft, she conceded, "But our parents would never forgive us. Why doesn't your sister move her wedding to the Saturday? It's a far more sensible day for a wedding than a Friday. Half my friends can't come because they have to work, or collect children from school."

Keya explained, "Like me, my sister is Indian, and in our culture the priest sets the date of the wedding after considering the bride and groom's horoscopes. He picks a day where the stars align, which is most favourable to the couple."

Natasha smiled. Her perfect teeth were white. "How romantic. Tell me more about the wedding." She leaned against the doorjamb, a wistful look on her face.

"The groom arrives at the venue on a horse ..."

"A horse." Natasha laughed. A rich, golden sound which suited her. So why did Keya have the impression she hadn't laughed much recently?

"Yes, the groom rides a horse and his family dance around him to the beat of the drums," Keya explained.

"Dancing, drums and a horse. It sounds such fun," grinned Natasha.

"I'm sure your wedding will be wonderful, too."

"I doubt it. Ezra, my fiancé, and I have had little say in it. His parents are paying, so they've taken it upon themselves to organise everything, and I mean EVERYTHING. If you want to change the date, you'll have to speak to them. But I can tell you now, they won't."

Keya's chest tightened. It was the response she'd feared but expected.

Natasha smiled at her. "It must be nice for your sister having you to help her."

Keya blushed guiltily. She knew she had done very little to help her sister prepare for her big day. "Do you have any siblings?" she asked, to hide her guilt.

"A younger brother and sister. I'd hoped Naomi would come down here to help me, but she's been delayed by work in London." Natasha fiddled with three colourful beaded strands on her wrist.

"Are you here alone?" asked Keya. Somewhere in her head, an alarm bell jingled.

"Yes, but Ezra's not far away." She bowed her head. "But he's busy with work and wedding plans. I've only seen him once in the last week." Natasha looked up and her hand grasped the delicate gold heart hanging from a chain around her neck.

"Did your fiancé give you that?"

"Yes, when I saw him last week. He told me not to worry about all the stress and the theatrics of the wedding, and that once it's over, we can settle down to a quiet life, without everyone else interfering."

"I'm sure he's right," Keya comforted.

She felt her phone vibrate in her pocket. It was probably Zivah wanting an update.

On an impulse, Keya said, "I'm meeting up with some friends at the pub tonight, if you want to join us."

Natasha stepped back and Keya had the impression of a clam retreating as its shell closed.

"At least take my card." Keya removed a business card from a slot behind her warrant card and handed it to Natasha. "Just in case you need anything. Or just someone to talk to."

As the front door closed, and Natasha disappeared back inside, Keya felt a chill run down her spine, despite the warmth of the sun.

Her phone vibrated again. Removing it from her pocket as she retraced her steps along the garden path, she answered the call, "Hi, Zivah."

CHAPTER FOUR

When Keya answered her sister's second call, she decided not to tell her about her discussion with Natasha Nkosi, the other bride getting married at Charbury Castle Hotel on the same day.

Instead, she suggested they meet at Neigh Bridge Country Park, beside the lake of the same name.

Zivah was already waiting in the gravelled car park when she arrived.

Keya was the oldest of three sisters. Zivah was younger than her by four years, and Maitri, the youngest, had nearly completed her A levels in her final year at school.

"Hi, sis," Keya greeted Zivah, giving her a hug. "I've brought a small picnic, but let's walk and talk. There's a path around the lake, which will take us about forty-five minutes. Does that sound OK?"

"I need the exercise," Zivah replied, "and space to clear my head."

Zivah was not dressed for a walk, wearing a floaty summer dress which accentuated her narrow waist, but at least she had pumps on her feet, and not sandals. Her thick dark hair, with a slight wave, shone in the sunlight. Unlike poor Natasha Nkosi, Zivah carried the aura of a bride-to-be.

Holding the wooden handrail, Keya lead Zivah down four wooden steps to a gravel path which ran beside the lake. It was so peaceful, with a mother duck swimming in front of her ducklings and the long grass beside the path swaying in the slight breeze. Keya sucked in deeply, filling her lungs with the fresh air.

As the path widened, Zivah fell into step beside her and said, "Making plans for the wedding was so exciting to start with, but now I wish it was all over and I could just move in with Aadi and start our life together."

"Mum wouldn't approve of that," replied Keya.

"Which bit? Not having a lavish ceremony and showing me off to her friends and family, or living in sin with Aadi?"

Zivah giggled at the thought. Sex before marriage wasn't taboo for a modern Indian girl, but it wasn't encouraged, and it certainly wasn't discussed. Keya had never asked her sister about that side of her relationship.

Hesitantly she asked, "Have you and Aadi, you know ..."

Zivah laughed. "Of course, we have. But we're very careful and take precautions. Can you imagine Mum's reaction if I arrived at the wedding ceremony with a huge pregnant belly? If she didn't faint on the spot, she'd disown me. Or both."

Keya thought Zivah was right.

"But what about you, sis?" asked Zivah. "It's been ages since you had a man in your life."

"I know." Keya had come to terms with her job not being compatible with the image of a good, stay-at-home Indian wife. It was one reason for reducing her police hours and opening the cafe and deli. "I think it's the job. Not fitting for a wife. But what about you? Will you keep yours?"

"I hope so. HR does seem an acceptable, but not particularly exciting, or taxing job for an Indian wife. And the company is understanding about maternity cover and allows flexible working hours for mums. They need to be, as there are so many of them. And if we, a HR company, don't set a good example, how can we expect other companies to do so?"

"I'm glad you'll have your work," mused Keya. "Even when you make Mum happy and have at least five children."

Zivah playfully hit her sister on the arm. "Can you imagine? Two or three will be plenty for me."

As they passed a bank of colourful wildflowers, Zivah became serious and asked, "Did you find the other bride?"

"I did."

"And will she change her wedding date?"

Keya stared straight down the path to a small white and tan terrier that scampered from one side of the path to the other, searching and sniffing.

"I actually think she would, as she said she'd prefer her wedding to be on a Saturday so more of her friends could come. But the problem is her prospective parents-in-law."

"Dad said they're very much part of the Cotswold set and donate to loads of charities."

Keya stopped and stepped to one side, allowing the elderly man and his terrier to pass. She looked directly at Zivah and said, "I think we have to face up to not having the wedding at Charbury Castle Hotel on the 16th. Is there anywhere else you considered?"

Zivah's arms hung by her sides. "Everywhere else will be booked. The 16th is just over a week away. How can I possibly find a venue in time?"

"You never know," Keya consoled her. "Somewhere might have a cancellation. And besides, you have more chance with a Friday than a Saturday. We should start phoning round."

Keya and Zivah continued their walk and Keya steered the conversation away from the wedding. Instead, they discussed their childhood, and friends, and boyfriends. Keya was pleased to hear her sister laugh.

When they finished their walk, they collected the red spotty cool bag from Keya's car. A few older couples and mums with young children in pushchairs were already settled at the picnic benches overlooking the lake, but Keya and Zivah found a spare one.

Keya deposited the cool bag on the table and said, "You've a choice of hummus and vegetable sandwiches, or egg mayonnaise with chives." She pulled the Tupperware boxes out and removed their lids.

"This is lovely, sis. Such a treat to sit outside in the sun with a picnic and just relax," Zivah admitted.

"I'm afraid I do need you to write down the other wedding venues you liked, so we can start calling them."

Keya produced her small black police notebook, which she usually carried with her, as she was never entirely off duty, especially in her new role in the rural Cotswold community.

Zivah took a hummus sandwich and picked up Keya's pen. As she munched, she scribbled away. "Quite a few places, particularly the older manor and historic houses, refused to allow a fire, even outdoors." Zivah crossed a name off her list.

Part of an Indian wedding ceremony involved the couple walking around an open fire seven times.

"I liked some of the converted Cotswold barn venues, but Mum didn't. She said barns are for animals, not people. And she also discarded any venues which were primarily pubs, however attractive they were. So that rather narrows our options." Zivah scored through several more names on the notepad.

Staring at the remaining names, she said, "I'll call Kiftsgate Court first."

"Are you happy speaking to them, or would you prefer me to call them?" Keya asked.

"This is my problem, so I'll do it," Zivah replied, squaring her shoulders and taking a deep breath.

When her call was answered, Zivah explained the double bookings and although Keya could discern a sympathetic voice on the other end of the phone, she knew from Zivah's slumping shoulders that the answer was no.

"Do you mind calling the next one?" asked Zivah. "That was harder than I expected."

Keya called four more venues which Zivah had noted down, but they either had weddings on the Friday or said they couldn't accommodate one as they were decorating and preparing for large ceremonies on the Saturday.

"Any more ideas?" asked Keya when she finished the last call.

Zivah shook her head dejectedly.

Keya leaned across the wooden picnic table and laid a hand on Zivah's arm. "We'll think of something." She returned the Tupperware container to the cool bag and removed the bar of Dairy Milk. "Chocolate always helps in these situations."

Keya spent another hour with Zivah, who didn't want to go home and face her parents. But then Aadi called, and Zivah broke down as she told him what had happened.

"I don't know what to do and our parents are going to be so disappointed," sobbed Zivah.

She had speakerphone mode on, so Keya heard Aadi reply, "This is our big day, nobody else's. We'll figure something out, won't we, Keya?"

"That's what I said. We will find a solution."

Zivah left to meet up with Aadi and Keya wondered what to do with the few hours she had before her fit-out meeting. It hardly seemed worth driving home.

She searched the internet and remembered a popular farm shop and cafe located nearby. She'd go for a cup of tea and a look round, for research purposes, and prepare for her meeting.

CHAPTER FIVE

Keya arrived at Akemans at a quarter to six. After the previous night's rain, it was a pleasant, barmy evening. Perfect for sitting outside the pub for a drink and a catch up with friends later.

She parked in the gravel car park in front of the antiques centre and walked round the adjacent single-storey stone building which housed the auction house. At the back of it, a line of tall metal fencing panels separated the cafe and deli building site from the public areas.

One of the mesh fence panels was open, so Keya walked through, striding towards the single-storey brick extension, from which Gilly Wimsey appeared.

"What a fantastic space," Gilly enthused. "I was worried how small it looked when it was being built, but now the walls and roof are complete, it's much larger inside. Have you worked out your layout?"

Keya felt her cheeks flush, but she held Gilly's gaze as she said, "I've decided to wait and concentrate on the cafe first. And Ryan suggested I trial products in the cafe, so I'll know what customers like when I'm ready to open the deli."

Gilly nodded in understanding as they entered the deli building. "That sounds sensible, and you won't have the expense of extra staff out here. But we do need to decide where to put plug sockets. If you install fridges and freezers, you'll need lots of them. And I think we should paint the space. Any idea what colour?"

"Creams, heritage greens and greys seem popular," Keya replied hesitantly. She was beginning to feel outside her comfort zone and was relieved she'd done some research by visiting the farm shop this afternoon and looking at others online.

"A warm cream sounds nice to me," said Gilly. "Bright and cheerful."

"Hello," said a young man, stepping inside. He was wearing a yellow hard hat and carrying a canvas briefcase over his shoulder. He had a folded construction plan in his hand.

"Is one of you Keya?" Keya judged the man to be in his mid to late twenties. He wasn't particularly tall and he had a relaxed, bright, even eager expression.

When Keya didn't answer, Gilly said, "This is Keya, and I'm Gilly. I run the antiques centre and my family owns the property."

The man shifted the building plan, securing it under his arm, so he could offer Gilly his hand. "I'm Daniel Hirst. Call me Dan." He smiled. An open, sincere gesture.

Keya stepped forward and said, "Hiya. I'm Keya, and all of this is rather daunting for me."

Dan's smile broadened. "Don't worry, I understand that most people I work with are experts in their field but know very little about the fitting-out side. But I'm here to help. So tell me about your vision for the shop."

Encouraged, Keya said, "It's going to be a deli, and I want to sell local produce and gifts. But Gilly and I were just discussing that opening it and the cafe at the same time, when I'm still working for the police, is too much for me."

"For the police?" Dan raised his eyebrows.

Gilly replied, "Yes, we're lucky to have our own police officer on call. We needed her last month when ..." She faltered, and Dan's eyebrows rose even higher as his eyes widened.

"The point is," said Keya in a business-like tone, "that we only want to do the bare minimum in here, so that I can start the deli later, probably in the autumn, and concentrate on the cafe for now."

"Understood," said Dan nodding, and appearing to accept Keya's dual roles of cafe and deli owner, and police officer. "But I prepared a few layout options if you'd like to look at them?"

"Oh yes," Gilly enthused.

Dan opened his briefcase and pulled out a thin plastic folder, which he handed to Keya.

She opened it and gasped. "Wow, Gilly, look at this." The first page showed a photographic 3D mock-up of the shop with products on shelves and open display fridges along the walls.

Gilly looked round the room. "Is there really room for all that in here?"

"When you optimise the space, you'll be surprised what you can fit in. But there are other, simpler layout plans, too."

Slowly, Gilly and Keya turned the pages as they considered other designs and layouts.

"Sorry, I'm late," Vic called as he entered the building.

Keya and Gilly ignored him as they discussed the contents of the folder. "All the plans have a counter over there," remarked Gilly, pointing towards the wall dividing the shop from the small office.

"And I like the metal stands," said Keya.

"They're extremely useful," Dan said, "as they are lightweight, durable, and the shelves can be adjusted. They're also easy to move, giving you maximum flexibility."

Gilly looked at Keya and said, "I think you should have some in the cafe to display your sample products, like Ryan suggested."

Keya agreed with Gilly. Turning to Dan, she asked, "What do you suggest I need to do now, so that I can easily start when I'm ready?"

"At the back of the folder you'll see a plan titled electrical layout. I recommend we undertake those works, install the sink, and possibly a chiller counter, if that's what you're going to use. And we should install the flooring and paint the walls and ceiling. Then you'll be ready to go."

Gilly looked at Keya and asked, "What do you think?"

"How much will it cost?" enquired Keya, as she knew she had to spend her budget sensibly.

"I'll work out the price. And I have a small, second-hand chiller counter if it's of interest."

"Definitely," replied Keya. "As long as it works."

"I've personally serviced and repaired it."

Vic stepped forward. "So Dan will prepare an estimate for the works in here. Shall we move on to the cafe space?"

As Vic had already installed kitchen equipment as part of the overall building works, the most complicated aspect of the cafe had already been dealt with.

As they entered the old mill, Gilly told Dan, "I've bought an eclectic collection of tables and chairs at recent auctions, but they should be all right to start with."

Keya didn't mind that none of the tables or chairs matched, as she'd also collected an assortment of vintage crockery and cutlery to use in the cafe.

She hung back as Gilly and Dan discussed flooring options. She was happy for the main walls to be painted cream and for the brickwork to remain exposed on the end wall, where large new windows had been installed overlooking the river and the space for the waterwheel.

Discussions continued between Vic, Dan and Gilly on lights, plug sockets, and aspects of the fit-out which Keya knew little about. As long as everything worked, and she could serve customers delicious food and drinks, she'd be happy.

After another ten minutes, Dan checked his watch. "OK, I'll revise my plans and provide budget estimates for the options we've discussed. Now, if you don't mind, I'm meeting up with an old college friend."

"That's sounds nice," said Gilly. "And thank you for coming. You've been a great help, hasn't he, Keya?"

"Oh, yes, definitely," Keya replied. He did seem to know what he was doing, but all she really wanted was for the building work to finish so she could get started.

As Dan left with Vic, Gilly remarked, "And I better collect the kids from Mum and Dad's. I hope Peter isn't home too late."

"Is he with a patient?" Keya asked.

"He has several in the village he needs to check on regularly at the moment. They all insist they've seen this ghost people are talking about, on the village green or floating along the river. It can't be true though, can it? Ghosts don't suddenly materialise, do they?"

Keya shrugged helplessly. "I've no idea. I'm just relieved not to be involved."

"Do you think someone is playing a trick?" Gilly drew her lips together.

"If they were, that would be a different matter." And one Keya suspected she'd be tasked to deal with. Then she smiled. "I also need to go and meet Aunt Beanie and the others at the pub."

CHAPTER SIX

Keya drove the short distance from Akemans to The Axeman pub, which fronted the main road running through Coln Akeman and looked out over the village green towards the River Coln.

Like most buildings in the village, it was constructed of Cotswold stone. A Virginia creeper covered part of the front wall and most of the side wall, which ran beside a narrow lane leading to the pub's rear car park and other houses in the village.

In autumn, the creeper's large, five-pronged leaves turned wonderful reds, yellows and oranges, but at the moment they were a fresh green.

Keya parked in the rear car park and walked back to the front of the pub where she'd spotted her friends sitting at one of the outdoor tables.

Ryan stood up as she approached. At work he was PC Ryan Jenkins, the youngest, and possibly the brightest of their team. Tall yet boyish, he grinned at Keya. "So you finally decided to join us," he joked.

"I'm not that late, am I?" Keya glanced down at her black watch.

A glass of orange juice and lemonade stood on the table beside an empty chair.

"No, he's only joking. I suspect he wants to order food," remarked

Ozzie Winters. Ozzie, with short, black, spiky hair, was a keen, resourceful and talented reporter.

She currently worked for the Cirencester Times, but as she wasn't even twenty yet, Keya wondered when the bright lights of London would lure her to one of the national papers, or perhaps she'd prefer to work for a glossy magazine.

"Hi, Keya," Norman Climpson nodded from the far end of the table. He'd trimmed his sandy coloured beard and, despite having a pint of his favourite Cotswold Gold standing on the table in front of him, his mouth was downturned and his voice dull and monotone.

Aunt Beanie sat beside him, but she didn't look up at Keya. Instead, she stared down at the table.

Hesitantly, Keya sat down in the empty chair, still looking at Aunt Beanie. Finally, the older woman glanced up, and Keya realised she'd been crying. Her skin was grey and her usually vibrant eyes were dull and puffy.

Keya gave her a sad smile, which Aunt Beanie returned.

"It's Cliff. He's caught a virus in the home, and he's been taken to hospital," Aunt Beanie explained. Cliff, or Uncle Cliff, as Keya knew him, was Aunt Beanie's husband. He'd spent his entire life at Meadowbank Farm until his dementia had become too much, and Aunt Beanie had finally agreed to move him to a local nursing home.

"How serious is it?" Keya asked in a concerned voice.

"It's not good," replied Aunt Beanie.

Norman sipped his beer and then said. "The difficulty is that, because he has dementia, the doctors won't give him fluids by IV drip to prolong his life, just painkillers. He has to be able to eat and drink on his own."

"It's awful," wailed Aunt Beanie. "His shrunken frame, just lying there."

Norman placed a hand on her arm and continued, "Because in late-stage dementia, the patient loses the ability to swallow and giving them fluids can actually fill up their lungs and cause huge discomfort."

"So every few hours the nurses are going to remove the drip and see if he'll drink some water. But what if he doesn't want any?"

Keya realised how scared Aunt Beanie was.

"I need to be with him."

"I know," agreed Norman, nodding slowly. "We'll finish our drinks, go back to the farmhouse so you can pack a bag, and then I'll drive you to the hospital."

Aunt Beanie sagged against the back of her chair.

There was an uncomfortable silence.

Ryan broke it by asking, "How did your meeting at the cafe go? What did you think about my suggestion for the deli?"

"That it was very sensible," replied Keya. "Dan, the fit-out guy, suggested we undertake some work, like electrics and decoration, so it'll be ready when I am. But for now, I'm concentrating on the cafe. Gilly was great and dealt with all the practical stuff. But I've so much to do before I open it."

"Keep it simple," remarked Aunt Beanie. "Most visitors to the antiques centre will just want a drink and a snack. A few will appreciate lunch, but nothing too elaborate."

Keya decided she'd spend the rest of the week organising her menu.

"Come on," said Norman, draining his glass. "We should go."

Aunt Beanie stood up and said, "Sorry to ruin the party."

"I'm sorry about Uncle Cliff," replied Keya.

Ozzie and Ryan murmured in agreement.

"I hope things improve at the hospital." Keya watched Norman escort Aunt Beanie around the side of the pub, and she was just about to sip her drink when two people walked past. She did a double take as she looked up at them.

Dan, her shop-fitting expert, was escorting the tall, attractive bride-to-be, Natasha Nkosi. Was she his friend from college?

As they entered the pub, Ozzie leaned forward and whispered, "That's Natasha Nkosi. What's she doing here?"

"She's living in a cottage beside the green," replied Keya, puzzled by Ozzie's question. "Why? How do you know her?"

"I don't, but she's the face of Farmers Jewellers. They launched a new range last year, and she was the poster girl."

"I wonder if that's how she met her fiancé?" Keya pondered.

"Of course," Ozzie sat up, her eyes sparkling. "They're getting married. But it's all a huge secret."

"What is?" Keya was struggling with the conversation.

"The wedding. Where and when it is."

"But it's Friday 16th June, and they're holding it at Charbury Castle Hotel, where my sister's supposed to be getting married."

"Supposed to be?" queried Ryan.

"The hotel double booked. I hadn't realised Natasha's wedding was such a celebrity event. There's no way they're going to move it. Poor Zivah. We tried our best today, but we can't find an alternative venue."

"Oh, I'm so sorry," commiserated Ryan.

"But how do you know about the wedding?" asked Ozzie.

"Zivah's?"

"No, Natasha Nkosi's."

"Because I spoke to her today. Although she said her fiancé's family has done all the organising."

The front door of the pub opened, and Dan walked out and looked round. There were no empty tables.

Dan spotted Keya and walked over to her, followed by Natasha. "Are these seats empty?" he asked.

"Yes, our friends just left," Keya replied.

Ryan stood up and, indicating to the seats, said, "Please, join us."

Before Dan sat down, he said, "I'm Dan, and this is my friend, Tasha."

Keya smiled at Tasha and said, "We met this morning."

Dan's smiled wavered, but he sat down at the end of the table as Tasha pulled back the chair next to Keya.

After a brief, uncomfortable silence, Keya looked at Dan and said brightly, "Thanks for your help today. It's hard enough organising my cafe menus, without having to work out where to put the plugs."

Dan smiled back. "I know, which is why I offer solutions rather than expecting clients to just provide me with layout plans."

Tasha turned to Keya and in her rich voice asked softly, "Did you sort out your sister's problem?"

Keya shook her head. "I'm not sure what we're going to do. But we'll think of something."

"I'm sorry I couldn't be more help. But as I told you, I have very little say in the wedding arrangements." Tasha gazed down at her glass of what Keya presumed was tonic, with either gin or vodka.

"You must be excited about your own big day," said Ozzie.

Tasha looked up at her and shook her head. "I wish it was over. All this fuss about who's sitting where, and what colour the napkins should be. It's ridiculous. And …" Tasha faltered and considered her glass again.

When she didn't continue, Ryan asked, in his boyish manner, "Where did you two meet?"

"At college," replied Dan, finally taking his eyes off Tasha and visibly relaxing. "We both took an interior design module. Tasha advised me on the creative side, like colours and soft furnishings, and I helped her with the practical elements."

"We made a good team." Tasha smiled wistfully at Dan. "And then we joined the real world."

"But you've enjoyed London, haven't you?" Dan sounded concerned.

"It has been fun. I love my job, and the modelling on the side was a bonus. But I've had to give all that up."

"Why?" asked Ozzie.

Keya could feel her reporter radar detecting the hint of a story.

"To get married. There were so many rows with Ezra's parents, that Ezra suggested I did as they asked, and resigned my job. Ezra's family still want me to model for Farmers Jewellery, for nothing of course, but once we're married Ezra said he'd help me find a new job. He's thoughtful that way. Unlike everyone else."

Tasha's face clouded over.

"It doesn't sound like the fairy-tale wedding the papers are making it out to be," commiserated Ozzie.

"Are these things ever what they appear to be? Sometimes I think I'd be happier running away from it all, or …" Tasha's voice faded as she returned to stare at her drink.

Ryan cleared his throat and asked, "What does everyone think of the ghost?"

Dan laughed.

But Tasha started and knocked the table, spilling her drink. "What ghost?" She asked in a shaky voice. Her own olive skin had lost its colour.

"The one haunting Coln Akeman," Ryan said, excitedly.

Tasha pushed back her chair and, without saying a word, turned and ran across the road.

A small white car screeched to a halt and Dr Peter Wimsey climbed out. He stared at the retreating figure of Tasha and then turned towards Keya's table.

"Who was that?" he called. "She didn't even look. I could have killed her." His face was as white as a ghost.

CHAPTER SEVEN

The following morning, Keya woke up just before her seven o'clock alarm. She usually woke earlier in the summer, especially when sunshine penetrated her bright tropical-themed curtains with their pink flamingo design.

But today she closed her eyes, trying to recall the idea she'd had at four o'clock in the morning.

She'd been dreaming about ghosts in Charbury Castle Hotel and then the hotel had changed to Windrush Hall. That was it. She'd contact the owner of the hall, Jay Newton, and see if he'd lend them his house for the wedding.

Wide awake, she sat up and called Zivah.

"Sis, are you my new alarm clock or something?" asked Zivah. "You needn't worry that I'm too depressed to get out of bed in the morning."

"I have an idea about your wedding venue."

"You do?" Zivah sounded alert. "What?"

"You remember how I helped organise that charity triathlon last summer?"

"The one where someone died?"

Keya ignored the comment and continued, "And the Christmas Ball ..."

"Where someone else died."

Irritated, Keya responded, "Neither of those was my fault, and nobody was even injured at the charity tabletop sale I organised in the spring."

"Fair enough," Zivah conceded. "So what?"

"They were all held at Windrush Hall. Why don't we ask Jay if we can use it for your wedding?"

"You mean the semi-retired rock star? I thought he was a recluse and didn't hire out his house."

"He's not that much of a recluse. He just values his privacy. And he didn't actually send Tracy, his man, to threaten that digital journalist with a shotgun. Although even without a gun, Tracy frightens me."

Retired rock star, Jay Newton, had bought Windrush Hall, a large house and estate in the Cotswolds, just over a year ago, and had moved from London to live there with his friend and music producer Tracy Ivers.

His presence in the Cotswolds hadn't passed without incident, as Zivah had pointed out, so he was careful about who he allowed on his property. But Keya knew from experience that he wanted to be part of the local community and help where he could.

"What do you think, sis? Surely, it's worth a try."

Zivah hesitated before replying.

"Is there something else?" asked Keya.

Another silence, before Zivah said slowly, "It's Aadi's parents. They're muttering about our wedding being cursed. Aadi told me to ignore them, but I can't. We had supper with them last night, so we could explain what had happened and, when we had, Aadi's mum started mumbling in Hindi. And his dad insisted on calling the priest after supper. When I left, they told me they had to consult the stars."

"The priest already consulted the stars and chose the 16th, so please don't worry." But Keya knew how superstitious some Indians were about bad omens and the spirits.

"Why don't I call Jay and see if we can at least visit Windrush Hall? And if you like the venue, and Jay is willing to host your wedding, we can take it from there. Let's face it, it doesn't matter what the spirits say at the moment, as you don't have anywhere to get married."

"Why are you always so practical and so … emotionless?"

"Emotionless? Me?" Nobody had called Keya that before.

"Sensible then."

Keya didn't think anyone had called her sensible either.

Zivah's voice softened. "And it's just what I need right now. Aadi is great, and, like you, trying to be pragmatic, but he has his family to deal with. And Mum is being a nightmare. In fact, can I come over and work from yours today?"

"Why?"

"I'm working from home at the moment, because of the wedding, but after yesterday I'm behind. And if Mum continues nattering at me and having hysterics, I'll never catch up. That way, if Jay does let us visit today, I'll be ready."

"OK, I'll see you soon."

I'd better get up too, thought Keya, and she wandered into the bathroom and switched on the shower.

Dressed and ready for the day, Keya descended the stairs and entered her kitchen. Although she'd eaten supper at The Axeman the previous evening, she still needed to wash up yesterday's teapot and tidy up before Zivah arrived.

Pouring the last of the milk into her coffee, she rinsed the container but realised her house plastics and metals recycling bin was full.

She'd sort it in a minute. First, she wanted to phone Aunt Beanie and check on Uncle Cliff at the hospital.

Aunt Beanie's phone rang and rang, and she was about to finish the call when Norman answered.

"Keya?"

"Norman, I wanted to see how you all were. It's such a difficult time for you."

"It certainly is," agreed Norman. "Beanie and I have been at the hospital all night. She wouldn't leave Cliff's side, and I wanted to be there for her. But I think we're through the worst.

Cliff sipped some tea this morning, and he asked for breakfast, which means the hospital can continue using the drip to administer his medicine and fluids. At least I think that's what's happening. Actually, Cliff was rather lucid and knew who Beanie was, which only made her cry again."

"I'm so glad he's on the road to recovery."

Keya heard another voice.

"I better go," said Norman. "Beanie and I need to get back to the farm to feed the animals and I'm dying for a change of clothes and a fry-up."

Smiling, Keya finished the call. She picked up the recycling bin and carried it along her hall to the front door. Unlocking the door, she continued outside to the small, covered area her neighbour and landlord, Derek, had installed beside the hedge which separated his front garden from hers.

The containers and tins rattled and clinked as she tipped them into the green council recycling box and a female voice called, "Is that you, Keya?"

It was Derek's wife, Peggy. In her 70s, she was the salt-of-the-earth type of person Keya loved meeting. Born in the Cotswolds, Peggy had moved to Keya's village of Ampney St Martin, five miles east of the historic town of Cirencester, in the early 1970s when she'd married Derek, a farm labourer.

Keya finished emptying her house recycling bin and moved out into the open, looking over the hedge at Peggy. "Hiya."

Peggy, overweight and with curly grey hair, placed a heavy looking blue-plastic laundry basket on the grass beside a washing line which stretched the width of her garden. Panting slightly, and red in the face, she wandered towards the hedge.

"Are you OK?" asked Keya. She knew Peggy was waiting for a heart consultation and possible surgery.

"I probably shouldn't be carrying the washing, but I've asked Derek that many times and he still hasn't done it, so it's easier to do it myself."

"All I wanted was a cup of tea," called Derek from the open front door. He was wearing a pair of blue-striped pyjamas and an old brown dressing gown and holding up a mug.

Keya heard a sharp bark and saw a flash of white.

"Hello Winston," said Peggy in a cheerful voice. "Have you finished your breakfast? Derek can take you out for a walk later. It'll do him good."

Keya had no idea who Peggy was speaking to, but she heard a rustle and looked down as a long white head with pointy ears poked out of the bottom of the hedge. With a final push, a small dog catapulted itself into Keya's garden.

"Winston," shouted Peggy.

Keya stepped back as the short-haired dog looked up at her with a quizzical expression.

"I'm so sorry, Keya," Peggy apologised. "We're looking after Winston for Derek's pal, Bernard, who's visiting his daughter."

"Anyway," said Peggy, ignoring Keya's pained expression as Winston started digging a hole in the lawn, "I was wanting to catch you. What's all this about a ghost in Coln Akeman?"

Keya groaned. She'd hoped the ghost story would fade away.

Peggy continued, "It's on the telly this morning. They're interviewing residents who say they've seen a woman in a white dress floating along the river."

Derek must have heard Peggy as he shouted, "That was your friend Marge, from the WI. You always said she couldn't see beyond her front gate."

Peggy scowled. "Take no notice of him. But is it true? Is there a ghost?"

"To be honest," confessed Keya, "I've kept out of it, as ordered. I have enough to deal with without chasing apparitions."

"It all sounds very spooky to me." Peggy looked down at her hands.

Keya waited. She heard a car drive slowly along the road on the far side of her garden gate.

"I have to go to hospital next week to meet my consultant. Derek should be able to drive me but …"

"Peggy, if you need me to drive you anywhere, just ask. And I keep a blue light in my Polo, so if it's an emergency I can, literally, give you a police escort." Although Keya didn't think cows, sheep or tractors, generally found locally on the country lanes, would take much notice of a flashing blue police light.

"Thank you." Peggy placed her hand on her chest.

Keya heard the squeak of her garden gate and glanced across as Zivah walked down the path.

"Is that your sister?" whispered Peggy. "She's very attractive. But so thin. It's not healthy."

Winston joyfully ran across to Zivah, who squatted down and patted his head.

"Are you going to stand there gossiping all day?" shouted Derek.

"I better go," muttered Peggy. "Can you pass Winston back over the hedge?"

Keya hesitated, but Zivah scooped Winston up in her arms and carried him across to the hedge, passing him into Peggy's waiting arms.

Peggy turned, put Winston down and walked across the garden, calling to Derek, "I don't see you putting the washing out to dry."

Keya picked up her recycling bin and said to Zivah, "That was quick."

"I skipped breakfast. Mum was unbearable. Do you have any fruit and yogurt?"

"Some," replied Keya hesitantly, thinking of her sparsely stocked fridge.

Back inside the house, Keya placed a piece of white bread in the toaster while Zivah hunted for muesli. She checked her watch. Was eight o'clock a sociable enough time to call Jay?

"Finally. This will have to do," exclaimed Zivah, walking through the back door from the rear utility room, which contained cupboards where Keya kept most of her dry foods, tins, and extra sauces. She was carrying a small box of cereal.

"Do you think it's too early to call Jay Newton?" asked Keya.

"Why? Is he one of those celebrity types who doesn't wake until lunchtime?"

"No. I'll phone him."

"Keya, lovely to hear from you," answered Jay. "I …". His voice faded away.

"Sorry, I didn't get that," said Keya.

"Just a minute."

Keya heard Jay shout, "Ringo" and then she heard birdsong. He must be out on his estate.

"Sorry about that," apologised Jay. "I'm taking my new springer spaniel, Ringo, out for a walk. He's so energetic and keeps chasing rabbits. Anyway, how are you? When are you opening your cafe? I heard about the delays."

"You mean the dead bodies? That wasn't great, but we're back on schedule, and the building work should be completed later this month." But would she be ready to open the cafe? Not unless she had time to herself to organise it. Still, Zivah's wedding was more important.

"Did you call for anything in particular?" enquired Jay.

"Oh, yes. Can my sister and I come round? We need to ask you a favour."

"Why can't you do it over the phone?"

"Zivah would prefer to speak to you in person."

"How very civilised. I'm in all day, although we're hosting a lunch and tour for Winchcombe Women's Institute."

"We'll drive straight over."

CHAPTER EIGHT

Keya drove Zivah to Windrush Hall in her reef-blue VW polo. It was a balmy summer day and, while she often complained about the road accidents uncut roadside verges caused, especially when drivers couldn't see round bends, she was enchanted by the wildflowers. Not that she knew any of their names.

"What a lovely day to be out," said Zivah. "Commuting between home and the office, I forget how wonderful the countryside is. But you must see it nearly every day."

"I suppose I do," Keya agreed. "And today is lovely, but it isn't always like this. To be called out to a farm in the middle of nowhere in the driving rain, or after a snowstorm, to deal with a stolen tractor or missing sheep, isn't much fun."

"I suppose not, but you're dealing with real people. Real lives."

"But aren't you? I thought that was what HR was all about. People."

"These days, it's all about rules and regulations. Who is allowed to say what to whom. What pronoun someone wants to be known by. That sort of thing. I'm not saying it isn't important to the individual, but it's a shame we have to legally prescribe how to act rather than people just behaving properly and courteously to each other. It's all about respect and common decency."

Keya agreed, but as a police officer, she'd seen her fair share of cruel and offensive behaviour. She turned off the road and drove between a pair of impressive stone pillars. The drive to Windrush Hall swept down before them.

Keya knew the house was not as old as some in the Cotswolds, but she always caught her breath when approaching it. She thought her friend, Dotty, had told her it was Georgian, but she only knew that meant it was built before Queen Victoria reigned. And although it was huge, it was well balanced, with a central front door and wings of rooms on either side.

To the right of the main house, there were more buildings, the old stables and stores, set around a central courtyard.

As Keya parked beside the steps leading up to the large front door, a brown and white springer spaniel with floppy brown ears bounded round the side of the house. It tried to jump up at Keya as she climbed out of her car.

"Ringo," called Jay. As he walked towards Keya and Zivah, he said, "Sorry, he's still young. I'm taking him to dog obedience classes, but I think we both have a long way to go." Jay looked at Zivah and smiled. "You must be Keya's sister. I'm Jay."

"Hi. Zivah. And what an amazing place you have."

Jay looked round proudly. The sun shone on the honey-coloured stone and a pair of large terracotta pots stood at the bottom of the steps, filled with vibrant flowers.

"Those are new," Keya observed, pointing to the pots.

"Tracy's idea. He thought we needed colour at the front of the house."

Keya turned back to Zivah, who was staring at Jay. Despite the warm day, he wore brown moleskin trousers, a long-sleeved checked shirt, and a tweed waistcoat.

Jay must have been aware of Zivah's scrutiny, as he said, "I have to dress the part of a country gent when I'm expecting visitors."

"You didn't dress up for us, did you?" asked Zivah, sounding aghast.

"No, it's for my WI ladies later."

A bald-headed man appeared at the top of the front steps and snorted.

"Tracy doesn't appreciate my opening up the house."

"I'd be less bothered if you did your own catering and set everything up," muttered Tracy.

He was the exact opposite of a country gent, wearing a black t-shirt with 'The Cure' printed across it and a pair of black jeans. "Keep that dog out of my garden," he called down. "It's just dug up my Sweet William."

Jay gave them a lopsided smile and said, "Let's go inside. We'll use the kitchen entrance if that's OK with you? Tracy doesn't like Ringo careering about the house. He has a tendency to knock things over."

Zivah gave Keya a sideways glance.

"I know," sighed Keya. "Just like me. But I'm clumsy, whereas Ringo is a pure bundle of energy."

As they walked across the front of the house, Zivah craned her neck to stare through the large sash windows.

"Zivah," hissed Keya.

"That's the dining room," said Jay, before whistling to Ringo whose head had disappeared round the back of a wooden tub of flowers at the entrance to the courtyard.

Keya liked Jay's kitchen. After he'd bought the house, Dotty had helped him convert the kitchen back to an open plan country-style one with a large, central, circular pine table and a racing green Aga range cooker.

They'd ripped out a storeroom and exposed the fireplace at the end of the room. It now housed a wood-burning stove around which several mismatched armchairs were arranged.

Ringo galloped across the flagstone floor and stuck his head around the side of an armchair.

Keya and Zivah jumped at a shrieking and hissing sound. Ringo reversed quickly, and as he sped across the kitchen to a plump circular dog bed beside the Aga, Keya noticed a drop of blood on his nose.

"I don't know when he'll learn that Inside Cat is the boss in here, and doesn't like to play when she's sleeping."

"Inside Cat?" queried Zivah.

"Keya will tell you all about her while I put the kettle on."

Keya explained, "When Jay and Tracy moved here, they realised they needed a cat to control all the mice who thought the house a great home, particularly during the cold winter months. So Dotty decided we should re-home a rescue cat, but instead of the cute, furry cats I liked, she spied a pair of tabbies which were cowering in the corner of their cage. They were both bald headed where someone had shaved off their fur. They did look really sad."

Jay removed the matching racing-green kettle from the Aga and continued, "So the girls brought the cats back here, but one immediately escaped outside. Which is how they acquired their unusual and somewhat unimaginative names of Inside Cat and Outside Cat. They're both excellent mousers and neither will take any nonsense from Ringo."

When they'd all got hot drinks, they sat down at the circular kitchen table.

Jay placed his hands on the table and looked from Keya to Zivah as he asked, "What's so important that you needed to drive over here to talk to me today?"

"It's my wedding," blurted Zivah. "The venue we booked has cancelled. They have another, more important one that day." Zivah gulped and looked down at the table.

"I'm so sorry. And I presume," Jay looked at Keya, "you thought this might be a suitable alternative."

Zivah looked up, tears in her eyes, and cried, "We phoned round loads of places, but they're either holding or preparing for weddings and don't have room for us."

"Steady," said Keya softly.

Zivah sniffed. "Sorry, I promised I wouldn't get emotional but …" her voice trailed off.

"It is a very important day for you," suggested Jay.

Zivah nodded her head.

"When are we talking about? August, September?"

"June. June the 16th," Zivah replied, her voice taut with emotion.

Jay raised his eyebrows and Keya caught a look of alarm on his face before he quickly composed his expression and said, "That is soon. No wonder you're so upset and desperate for an alternative venue. I'm happy to help out, but we don't have room for many guests inside. We hired a marquee for the Christmas ball, didn't we, Keya?"

"That's true," agreed Keya.

"And I don't know if it will be any easier finding a marquee than an alternative venue at this time of year."

"But we could at least try," Zivah pleaded.

"Of course you should. Keya has the details of the company we used at Christmas." Jay looked at Keya for confirmation.

"I'll have to look, but I'll have their contact details somewhere." Keya turned to Zivah and said, "But I think you should explain to Jay exactly what happens at an Indian wedding. I doubt he's attended one."

"We're planning the wedding ceremony to be in the afternoon. My fiancé will arrive riding a horse with his family dancing around him to the beat of a drum. If it's acceptable, my family will greet them at the front door."

Zivah's eyes shone, and she looked at Keya. "Can you imagine Mum and Dad standing at the top of the steps with Aadi's family gathered below? And we could decorate the steps with flowers."

"What happens to the horse? It doesn't come inside, does it?" asked Jay, in a wary tone.

Zivah laughed. "No, the person we hire it from takes it away. After my parents complete the ritual of washing my fiancé's feet, they will lead him and his family to the location of the main ceremony. This will be in a mandap, which is a covered structure with pillars. Aadi and I exchange garlands, the priest chants and we walk around the fire."

"Fire?" enquired Jay.

"Yes, there's a small fire which represents Agni, the Fire God. He dispels darkness and ignorance in life, leading to eternal light and knowledge."

Jay asked hesitatingly, "So do you intend the ceremony to be indoors or outside?"

"Outside," laughed Zivah. "No venue allows open fires inside."

Jay smiled slowly with relief.

"And then there's lots of eating and dancing after the ceremony," added Keya.

"As there should be at such a joyous event." Jay sat back and smiled.

"The house is yours, to greet your groom and his family, and I can offer you the use of the garden for your ceremony and party. But it's up to you to find a marquee and organise the caterers and all the other trappings of the wedding. And can I ask that you clear up every scrap of litter and broken glass afterwards, so we don't upset Tracy."

"Oh wow. Thank you." Zivah jumped up and hugged Jay. "I'm going to get married after all."

CHAPTER NINE

As Keya drove up the drive away from Windrush Hall, Zivah chatted at her excitedly.

"We can decorate the hall and the front room looking out over the garden. Our family can wait there, and we can provide them with refreshments."

Jay had given Zivah a quick tour of the house before his WI visitors arrived and she'd continued to talk enthusiastically about it and her wedding since the moment they'd climbed back into Keya's car.

Keya smiled indulgently at her sister as she passed between the stone pillars and braked to a stop. She was just checking if the road was clear when her phone rang. Looking at the caller ID, she groaned. It was her boss, Inspector Evans.

She didn't answer the call with her usual enthusiasm. "Hello, Inspector," she said warily.

"Sergeant Varma. I'm sorry to bother you." The inspector's Welsh baritone voice did indeed sound apologetic.

"Sergeant Onion …"

Keya winced. She knew her colleague, Sergeant Nick Unwin, was not popular at Cirencester Police Station, as many officers saw him as pushy and ambitious. And she'd been annoyed with him for arresting her friend, Dotty, for crimes everyone knew she couldn't have committed. But for their boss to continue using his derogatory nickname …

"… is away on another course. This one's about dealing with the press and public during an investigation. Which is ironic, as he'd gain some valuable hands-on practice if he were here."

Inspector Evans cleared his throat. "I know you're not on duty this week, but would you mind popping down to Coln Akeman and meeting up with PC Jenkins? The locals are complaining about the interest this ghost is causing, particularly after the story aired on national TV this morning."

Keya remembered Peggy telling her she'd seen the ghost story on her telly.

"But what about the Chief Constable's order?" enquired Keya.

"That related to the ghost. This is about people. We need to maintain the peace and make sure nobody trespasses or injures themselves searching for the phantom."

"OK," Keya agreed wearily. She'd really wanted to help Zivah contact marquee companies, but she felt a responsibility to keep the inhabitants of the Cotswolds safe, even from themselves.

Finishing the call, Keya turned left and said, "I have to make a slight detour to Coln Akeman and make sure there's no trouble."

"Why should there be?" asked Zivah.

"Because the public and the press are descending on the village for a ghost hunt."

"A what?"

"I'm sure there's a perfectly reasonable explanation for ghost sightings in the village, but the Inspector wants me to check that everyone is behaving themselves."

"Why wouldn't they be?"

"We've had a few instances recently where members of the public have gone further than just helping us with our enquiries. There are those that call themselves digital detectives. I have to admit, it's amazing what they find out using information openly available on the internet, and I know Ryan has developed some contacts with them. But a few go too far, interfering with crime scenes and bothering vulnerable people impacted by police investigations. The amateur detectives film themselves and post on social media."

"Sounds like attention seekers," remarked Zivah.

"I'm afraid that's exactly what they are. But a few have huge followings. And they make it much harder for us police officers to do our jobs."

As Keya drove slowly into Coln Akeman, she realised how quickly the ghost story had blown up. She couldn't even see the village green for outdoor broadcast production trucks parked face on to the green and obstructing the road.

Parked cars lined the street, with their inhabitants standing around in groups on the pavements and in the road.

"Ryan's first job is going to be crowd control, and making sure nobody is hit by a frustrated local trying to drive through the village."

"Where are you going to park?" asked Zivah.

"I'll try the car park at the back of the pub."

As Keya had suspected, the newcomers weren't aware of the pub car park and she easily found a space.

She opened the back of her car and removed a spare luminous police jacket she kept for emergencies, and a flat-topped black police hat with a black and white checkerboard band around it.

As Keya and Zivah walked out of the car park towards the main road and the village green, Zivah asked, "Won't people notice that you're wearing jeans?"

"Probably not, but it doesn't matter. I don't always wear my uniform as the Rural Engagement Officer. But I thought the jacket and hat would give me some authority today, especially as I'm responsible for Ryan as his senior officer."

As they reached the main road, Keya spotted Ryan's capped head above the crowd of people surrounding him. Many were holding rods with microphones attached and they were pushing them at Ryan's face.

Keya took a deep breath and whispered, as much to herself as to Zivah, "Wish me luck."

She strode across the road and addressed the group surrounding Ryan. "Ladies and gentlemen. This is not a crime scene and we, the police, do not have a statement to make. We are here purely to ensure you act in a responsible manner and are respectful to the inhabitants of Coln Akeman."

A TV camera turned towards Keya and a woman shouted, "What do you know about the Weeping Widow?"

Keya had never heard of the Weeping Widow. Was that the name someone had given the ghost?

"As I said, I am here purely to ensure public safety, which starts with moving all these lorries and parking them side on so as not to restrict the flow of traffic."

"But this is a news story," the woman cried.

"And there'll be another one if someone is knocked over by a frustrated motorist, or there's a head-on collision as drivers negotiate round your trucks."

Despite plenty of muttering, the crowd around Ryan dispersed and lorry engines started up.

"That was amazing, sis," said Zivah. "I didn't know you could be so authoritative."

"Neither did I." Keya felt her legs shaking.

"Thanks, Keya," said Ryan as he strode over to join them. "I was completely swamped."

"I could see. This is my sister, Zivah," Keya introduced.

Zivah smiled.

"The one who's getting married?" Ryan asked hesitantly.

Zivah's smile broadened. "Yes, and Jay Newton has just offered us the use of Windrush Hall."

Ryan looked at Keya and said, "So you did think of something?"

Keya nodded. "Jay's letting us use Windrush Hall, but we still need to find a marquee, and arrange the food and flowers."

"Keya, I think someone wants to speak to you," said Zivah. "There's a lady over there waving her arm."

They all turned to look across the village green at the cottages facing it.

"That's Natasha Nkosi," said Ryan.

"The other bride!" exclaimed Zivah.

"Yes, and I should make sure she's OK," said Keya. "She left the pub in such a hurry last night that Dr Peter nearly ran her over."

"You speak to her," suggested Ryan, "while I supervise these TV trucks and make sure they park somewhere sensible."

Keya strode across the green to the path that ran alongside it. As she reached Tasha, she realised Zivah had followed her. She was about to tell her sister to go back when Tasha spoke.

"What's going on? Is this about me?"

Keya's initial thought was how self-centred this young woman was, but perhaps this sort of thing happened when you were a famous model.

"No," she replied. "There have been sightings of a ghost and the story broke on the news this morning."

"A ghost?" Tasha's olive-toned skin had a grey tinge, and her eyes were red and puffy. She'd been crying.

"Yes, I think they're calling her the Weeping Widow, but I'm sure there's no such thing. Probably some prank by the local kids, which has got out of hand."

Zivah stepped forward and, tilting her head at Tasha, asked in a soft voice, "Are you OK? You've been crying."

Tasha sniffed and rubbed her eyes. "It's nothing," she said dismissively. "Just pre-wedding nerves."

"Tell me about it," cried Zivah. "And I have to re-arrange mine."

Tasha's eyes widened. "Are you the other bride? The one who was supposed to be getting married at Charbury Castle Hotel?"

Zivah nodded.

"I'm so sorry. If I could change my wedding date, I would, but my parents-in-law ..."

"Don't worry," interjected Zivah. "I know all about parents-in-law. Mine are trying to stop my wedding, as they say it's cursed."

"It's what?"

Keya backed away, leaving Zivah and Tasha to discuss their weddings and the issues they were both having. She thought it would be good for Tasha to have someone else to talk to. Keya didn't think it was good for her being on her own at the moment.

Keya wandered back across the green and re-joined Ryan. "So what is this Weeping Widow ghost everyone's looking for?"

"I saw it last night."

"You what? Are you sure?"

"Yes, Ozzie and I both did. We stayed in the pub for another half hour or so after you'd left, and it was dark when we walked out the front door. We crossed the road to our cars, parked beside the green, and that's when Ozzie saw it and nudged me. A woman with long hair wearing a white dress floating along the riverbank."

"Did you get a photo?"

"I tried to, but she was too far away." Ryan handed Keya his phone, but she could only see patches of light and dark. "I might try to enhance it, but I'm not sure it will work."

Keya stepped back and exclaimed, "So you started this news frenzy?"

"Me? No. I drove home to Meadowbank Farm. I had a cup of hot chocolate with Norman, who's worried about Uncle Cliff and Aunt Beanie, and went to bed." Ryan paused, and Keya could tell he was thinking. "But Ozzie might have. If she wrote a story about it."

Ryan took his phone back and scrolled through it. "Yes, here it is. She posted her story online at midnight."

"For that," Keya declared, "you get to stay here for the rest of the day to make sure everyone behaves themselves."

"Where are you going?"

As Keya strode across the village green, she shouted back, "To organise a wedding!"

CHAPTER TEN

As Keya strode across the village green, she spotted a man in a lightweight blue rain jacket standing at Tasha's front door. Was he speaking to Tasha or Zivah? And what did he want?

He turned away from the door, which closed, walked down the garden path, and entered the garden of the next cottage along. He knocked on the door, which opened as Keya arrived at Tasha's garden gate.

Holding up a phone, he said, "Hello, my name's Gareth Cook, and I'm investigating the Weeping Widow ghost. Have you seen her?"

Keya couldn't hear the occupant's reply, but as the door began to close, Gareth shoved his foot in the door and demanded, "The public has a right to know."

Keya didn't know who lived in the cottage, but it was possible they were elderly or vulnerable and Gareth's behaviour was unacceptable.

Sighing, she left Tasha's gate and walked down the path of the neighbouring cottage.

"Sir, please take your foot out of the door."

Gareth hastily obeyed and as he turned to Keya, still holding up his camera, the front door of the cottage slammed shut.

"Officer, I'm only exercising my rights as a member of the public.

People have the right to know what's going on when there's been a cover-up."

"And what is being covered up?" asked Keya politely.

"The Weeping Widow. Her appearance means she's seeking revenge for her unlawful death. And if the police won't investigate it, I will."

"Sir, this is private property. Please leave." Keya walked back down the garden path.

Gareth followed her, asking questions. "Have any bodies been discovered in the village? Have there been any mysterious disappearances?"

Keya put her hand up in front of Gareth's phone and replied, "Nothing I'm aware of. Now please conduct your business without intruding on the inhabitants of Coln Akeman."

Keya was used to dealing with the press, who usually followed a code of conduct, but not with digital detectives and sleuths, or whatever they called themselves. And they didn't appear to follow any rules, legal or moral.

Irritated, she walked down the path to Tasha's door and used the rose-shaped door knocker to rap on it.

The door opened an inch and Zivah called out, "It's OK. It's just my sister."

Removing her cap, Keya entered the cottage.

It was neat and tastefully decorated. A jam jar of wildflowers on the hall table seemed out of place amongst the carefully designed cottage chic.

Zivah led Keya into a cosy living area. A tray holding a cafetiere, a jug and some cups, was balanced on what looked like a large leather footstool between two floral sofas.

"Would you like a coffee?" Zivah asked.

"Yes, please." Keya sat down on the sofa, facing Tasha.

"Tasha and I have been comparing stories about weddings and relatives. And I thought having Indian parents was tricky."

Tasha was staring at Keya wide-eyed.

"Oh, yes, as I said yesterday, I'm a police officer. I was called to sort out all the TV crews and press obstructing the road and annoying the villagers."

Tasha relaxed but didn't say anything.

"Where do your parents live?" Keya asked politely.

"London, but they're on their way down to see me. I've no idea what they'll think of all the TV crews. Probably that they're here for me, and I've done something stupid or newsworthy."

"Why would they think that?" enquired Keya.

"No reason," lied Tasha as she glanced towards the hall. "Just that they won't believe a ghost story is more important than my upcoming wedding. But I guess all parents get wrapped up in their daughters' weddings."

Was that really the reason? Keya wondered.

"Is your sister coming with them?" she asked.

"No, I spoke to her last night, and she said she'll really try to be here by Saturday or Sunday. I hope she does ..." Tasha's voice trailed off.

Zivah handed Keya her coffee and sat down next to her on the floral sofa. She said, "And tonight Tasha has to face her in-laws. And so do I. Aadi's just sent me a message."

Keya wondered if this was one of the reasons she'd avoided marriage. You didn't just take on a husband, but a whole other family. And what if they didn't like you, or think you were good enough for their precious son?

Keya watched Tasha fiddle with the gold heart hanging around her neck. "How are you sleeping?" she asked.

Tash looked at her. Was that alarm or fright in her eyes? She bowed her head and replied, "Not great. I usually go for a walk in the evening before bed."

Keya hoped she didn't bump into the Weeping Widow. But there again, at the moment, she didn't know whether Tasha or the ghost would be most alarmed by the encounter.

"And does that help?" pressed Keya.

"Sometimes. I can't help waking in the middle of the night and thinking about all the things I haven't done. And all the things I have." She tugged at her purple-patterned cotton blouse.

Keya removed a spare notepad from her pocket, and looking up the details on her phone, wrote down a number and an email address.

Tearing the sheet out, she held it up and said, "This is the number for the Samaritans. If you feel overwhelmed, alone, or you just don't know what to do, call them. Or you can email if that's easier. But the Samaritans are great, and used to speaking to people who are finding life hard."

Zivah grabbed the paper and Keya's pen and scribbled something. "And this is my number. If your wedding plans, your in-laws, or your family are too much, give me a call. I do understand what it's like organising a wedding." Zivah held the paper out.

Tasha took it and, smiling sadly, said, "Thank you. But in the end, this is my problem. Now if you don't mind, I think I need to lie down before my family descends."

Zivah stood up and reached for the coffee tray.

"Don't worry, I'll do that … later," said Tasha, listlessly.

"It's no problem." Zivah carried the tray through to what Keya presumed was the kitchen.

She returned as Keya said, "Don't feel you're alone in this. You're not. You have my card and Zivah's phone number. Please reach out if you need us."

"Thank you," Tasha replied. She didn't stand up or escort Zivah and Keya to the front door.

"Good luck," called Zivah as they left.

Outside in the fresh air, Keya realised how stuffy the cottage had been.

As they walked down the path, Zivah said, "I'm worried about her. You should have seen the kitchen. All empty coffee cups and glasses which didn't smell as if they'd had water in them. And I peeked into the fridge and all it had in it was some milk, a bar of chocolate, and some out-of-date fruit and salad."

Keya opened the garden gate. "I know what you mean. But there isn't much more we can do. At least her family are joining her today which should cheer her up."

"I wish her sister would come down. They're very close and I know how grateful I've been for my sister's support." Zivah linked arms with Keya as they walked back across the village green.

CHAPTER ELEVEN

Loud, insistent knocking woke Keya the following morning.

"Keya, sis, let me in!"

Zivah! What did she want? And why was she banging on the front door so early?

Keya pulled herself out of bed, but the duvet wrapped itself around her and she fell onto the floor. "Oh toda!" she exclaimed as she untangled herself.

The knocking continued.

"I'm coming," Keya shouted.

Barefooted, she ran down the stairs, grabbed the key from a pot on the small hall stand, and unlocked the front door.

As she flung it open, she cried, "What's happened? Who's died?"

Zivah took a step back. "Why would you think anyone is dead?"

"Because of the racket you're making. What time is it?"

"Half past seven."

Had Keya slept through her alarm clock? No, she'd decided not to set it last night. She stepped back so Zivah could enter. "Go and put the kettle on while I sort myself out."

Keya returned upstairs. She didn't shower but dressed quickly, pulling on the jeans from the day before which she'd draped over a chair.

Downstair in the kitchen, Zivah was sitting at the kitchen table scrolling through her phone. Two cups of coffee were on the table beside her.

"So what's so urgent you had to race round here and wake me and half the village up?" Keya asked as she sat down, placing her phone on the table.

"It's only you I woke. Your neighbour waved at me from her open front door," Zivah said, sitting back and folding her arms.

"OK, so I had a lie-in today. What do you want to tell me?"

Zivah dropped her arms to her sides. "I think Aadi's parents want to postpone the wedding, or worse still, cancel it." Her voice rose in pitch.

Trying to remain calm, Keya replied practically, "You knew losing the venue worried them."

"I did, but when I turned up for supper last night, the priest was waiting. He took Aadi and me aside to go through our horoscopes again. When he left 'to consult the stars', he didn't look very happy. And Aadi's mum spent all supper telling us stories of marriages which had failed, supposedly because of things the bride did before the wedding."

"You know how superstitious some Indians can be. And would it be so terrible to move your wedding by a month or so? At least it would give us time to find another venue, or a marquee and caterers for Windrush Hall."

"But what about my lunch the day before? My friends have organised time off work or arranged for someone to look after their children."

Keya remembered that months ago she had requested the Thursday before the wedding off, as well as the Friday for the wedding itself.

"We could still go ahead with lunch even if the wedding date is moved."

"But it won't be the same!"

Keya picked up her coffee. She was going to need the caffeine to manage her sister this morning.

Her phone rang.

She checked the ID. It was Ryan.

"Hiya Ryan, you're not ghost hunting again, are you?"

"Very funny. But I am back at Coln Akeman. Think yourself lucky that the inspector called Nick off his course, deciding he could have some hands-on experience of dealing with the press this morning."

Keya was relieved she hadn't been called to Coln Akeman. But why was Ryan calling her? And so early?

"But I'm calling about something else. When I was walking around the village checking everything was in order, I found a cottage with the door wide open. I went inside and called, but nobody was there. It was all neat and tidy, and there was no sign of a burglary. But there was a phone lying on a leather ottoman."

An alarm bell rang in Keya's head. "Which property?" she asked.

"The one a neighbour said she saw you go into yesterday. Rose Cottage, it's called."

"That's Natasha Nkosi's. I'll come right over."

Keya finished the call and stared at Zivah.

"What's happened to Tasha?" asked Zivah.

"I'm not sure, but I need to find her and make sure she's OK."

"She's probably just popped out to the village shop," Zivah said.

"Is that what you really think?"

Zivah shook her head. "No. I'll come with you. I think she trusts me."

After changing into her spare police uniform, Keya drove Zivah to Coln Akeman, quickly, but carefully. She skidded to a stop at one point when a large Range Rover sped around a corner in the middle of the road.

Normally she'd have turned round and sped after it to give the driver a warning, but today she just wanted to get to Coln Akeman.

If anything, there were now even more outdoor production lorries and vehicles in the village than the day before. Keya pulled up alongside Ryan's squad car and jumped out. She felt Zivah follow her as she jogged down the path beside the village green to Tasha's cottage.

Ryan was talking to an elderly gentleman outside the first cottage.

Keya heard the words, "Kept to herself," and then "visitors" and "young men." She wondered who those young men were.

Zivah ran up the garden path and into Rose Cottage.

Keya waited. She looked at the cottage and slowly turned round, taking in the other houses in the row. The curtains of some properties twitched, but most occupants stood openly on their front doorsteps, either watching her and Ryan or looking towards the production vehicles.

Keya continued to turn around. The path beside the green led on towards the river where she knew it joined a well-worn footpath running along the riverbank from Akemans to the next village of Coln St Aldwyns.

As she turned further, she took in more houses facing the village green from the opposite side, and then the road which ran through the village. The Axeman was obscured by production lorries and groups of people standing around. Luckily, they didn't appear interested in the activity around Rose Cottage.

Ryan joined Keya and said, "Nobody's seen Natasha this morning. She had visitors yesterday afternoon and a young man visited her in the evening. They went out together, but nobody's sure if or when Natasha came back."

"But her front door hasn't been open all night, has it?"

"I'm not sure. I've only spoken to the neighbours on either side so far, and neither of them are the night-time party type."

Zivah walked out of Rose Cottage, shaking her head. When she reached Ryan and Keya, she said, "There's no sign of her. The bed's unmade, but I'm not sure that means anything. You saw the state of the cottage yesterday?"

"I didn't," said Keya, "but you told me about the kitchen."

"That's all been tidied up and someone's filled the fridge. But I think it's her phone in the living room. And someone like Tasha wouldn't go far without it."

"That's what I thought," Ryan agreed. "Which is why I called you." He looked at Keya and asked, "What should we do?"

"We shouldn't panic or start a national manhunt. You should continue as you were before, checking that none of the villagers have been harassed by reporters or over-zealous ghost-hunting members of the public. But drop into conversation that you're trying to trace the occupant of Rose Cottage, a young woman who recently came to the village, and ask casually if any of them have seen her this morning."

"What will you do?" asked Ryan.

"Zivah and I are going for a walk, along the river."

"You don't think she's fallen in, do you?" gasped Zivah.

"I hope not," replied Keya. "But if I needed to clear my head, that's where I'd go."

CHAPTER TWELVE

"Which way now?" asked Zivah as she and Keya reached the River Coln.

The river was about eight metres wide at this point and appeared peaceful as it flowed gently downstream.

On the opposite bank, the grass was kept short by sheep or cattle, and clumps of reeds, grasses and river plants grew out of the water. The section where they were standing had stone edging, and the path was paved with tarmac.

Keya looked from left to right, but there was no sign of Tasha. How long had she been out?

"We should stick together. Do you want to go left or right first?" she asked Zivah.

"It would be quicker if we split up," her sister replied.

"But what if something happens? Or you meet someone?"

"Who am I going to meet? I'm only looking for Tasha."

Was Keya's police brain making her think the worst might have happened? Or did she have a nasty feeling about this?

"If you're sure. But phone me as soon as you see Tasha, or anyone else for that matter. And be careful. We have no idea what has happened and who might be involved."

"Sis, calm down. I'm sure nothing has happened to Tasha. She left for a walk, to clear her head, and mistakenly left her door open."

Keya remembered that Tasha lived in London, and people there locked their doors and didn't leave them open, by mistake or otherwise. But she didn't want to dampen Zivah's enthusiasm with her doubts.

"You go right, towards Akemans, and I'll follow the path the other way towards Coln St Aldwyns. And remember, keep in touch."

"I will, I will," chorused Zivah as she set off excitedly along the river path.

Keya started in the opposite direction and saw that she wasn't the only person on the river bank this morning. A group of people were blocking her path, and she realised too late that they included a TV cameraman.

The crowd parted, and the woman who had complained to her the day before about moving her production lorry, called out, "Sergeant, are you looking for the Weeping Widow who was sighted again last night?"

"No, I'm patrolling the village, making sure the press and public aren't intimidating or annoying the inhabitants."

The woman scowled before demanding, "What are the police going to do about the ghost?"

Keya looked up at the sky. A few clouds lingered, so she said, "Maybe it'll rain and dampen its spirit."

Some members of the crowd moaned, but she heard one man laugh. Smiling, she manoeuvred around the group and continued her search for Tasha.

In front of her, a man slowly turned in a circle, holding out a device which looked like a cross between a police radio and a Geiger counter. Concentrating on the device, he walked steadily forward until he reached a garden fence.

As he started to climb over the fence, Keya called, "Hey, that's private property. You can't go round climbing into people's gardens."

"But I'm sure the Weeping Widow is there."

Keya looked at the bungalow's neat garden. "Is it hiding in the garden shed?" Beside the greenhouse there was a wooden shed with its door padlocked shut.

Keya waited until the grumpy man returned to the path.

"Don't let me catch you doing that again, or I will arrest you for trespassing." Keya knew she probably wouldn't. She could only justify such an arrest if the trespasser was breaching the peace and intending to harm the owner of the land or his property. But breaking into a locked shed would count.

Keya was still contemplating the legalities of members of the public entering other people's property when she realised she'd come to the end of the village. The tarmac path stopped beside a wooden bench, presumably built so weary walkers could rest and enjoy the peace of the riverscape before returning home.

And it was peaceful here. A weeping willow on the opposite bank dipped its branches into the water, which rippled as it flowed round them. A black and white cow mooed at its friends and a grey squirrel ran up the trunk of a tree on the edge of the wood which the river path entered.

But there was no sign of Tasha. And as Zivah hadn't called, presumably she hadn't found her either.

Keya followed the packed earth path through the wood and out the other side, where it continued along the side of the field. The river was narrower, and the banks overgrown. Stalks of red flowers swayed gently in the breeze.

Keya halted by a wooden stile as a couple walked towards her. They were in their late 50s but not dressed in the usual walking attire of strong boots and lightweight trousers.

They struck Keya as city people. The woman was wearing a blue and white dress, but at least she had pumps on her feet and not heels. The man, with ebony coloured skin, looked hot and bothered. He was wearing a pair of dark trousers, a long-sleeved shirt, and his navy blazer was draped across his arm.

They didn't look like walkers or ghost hunters.

The couple glanced up when they were about five metres from Keya and stopped. Their mouths fell open, and Keya caught looks of panic in their eyes.

Of course, if they were from the city, the sight of a police officer emerging from a wood in the middle of the country would be strange.

Even country folk would be concerned, as they usually only saw police officers at events or in the towns.

"Morning," Keya said as brightly as she could. "Have you walked from Coln St Aldwyns?"

"Yes, Officer. We're walking to see our daughter in Coln Akeman, but it's further than we thought. Still, an elephant walks many miles."

Keya wasn't sure why the man was talking about elephants, but the alarm bell in her head rang again. "Your daughter?"

"Yes, she's hired a cottage in the village before her wedding next week. It's nice for her to be somewhere quiet, away from London, to prepare for it."

"Your daughter wouldn't happen to be Tasha Nkosi, would she?"

"Why, yes?"

"What's happened?" cried the woman, stepping forward.

"Nothing, as far as we know. But Tasha's not in her cottage and she's left the door wide open. I thought she might have gone for a walk."

"She told us yesterday how much she enjoyed walking beside the river," said the man.

"She finds its quiet and soothing after London," added the woman.

"Are you Tasha's parents?" Keya enquired.

"We are. I'm Solomon Nkosi and this is my wife, Linda."

It looked as if Solomon wanted to shake hands as he stepped forward but halted awkwardly beside the stile.

"Why don't I walk with you to Coln Akeman?" suggested Keya. "I'm sure Tasha will be back by now and we can all enjoy a cup of tea."

"That sounds lovely," said Linda as she gripped the wooden posts supporting the stile and pulled her ample body up. Keya helped her balance as she negotiated the stile and arrived safely, if somewhat gracelessly, on Keya's side.

Solomon slowly followed, refusing Keya's help and turning round so he climbed backwards down from the stile.

As they entered the wood, Keya asked, "Are you staying until the wedding?"

"No, we return to London tomorrow, but we're back down next Wednesday and staying in the Charbury Castle Hotel for the wedding," Solomon answered.

Keya felt awkward. There wasn't room to walk two abreast along the path and she felt Solomon wanted to lead, but he was embarrassed as he didn't know where the path led. She strode on in front.

"And you saw Tasha yesterday?" Keya remembered Tasha telling her and Zivah that her parents were visiting from London.

"Yes, although I have to say I was surprised by all the news crews. The Cotswolds aren't as quiet as we expected. And there was nowhere to park. That's why we decided to walk this morning."

"And it's such a lovely day," said Linda.

Keya wasn't so sure about that. She'd been joking earlier about rain, but more clouds were gathering now.

"You must be very proud of your daughter," Keya said.

"As proud as a lion. My innocent little girl marrying an important man like Ezra Farmer." Solomon held his head high and joined Keya as they met the wider tarmac path.

Keya narrowed her eyes. Tasha hadn't appeared innocent, but perhaps it was a turn of phrase. She was pleased that the river path was clear of ghost hunters and reporters and that the first person they met was Zivah.

Her face was red, with beads of sweat clinging to her forehead. She had a haunted look as she said, "Tasha hasn't come back, and I can't find her anywhere."

CHAPTER THIRTEEN

Keya joined her sister Zivah on the bank of the River Coln and whispered, "These are Tasha's parents."

Zivah's eyes widened in understanding and Keya turned back to face Linda and Solomon Nkosi.

"This is my sister, Zivah. She's also getting married next week ..."

Keya felt Zivah flinch.

"She and Tasha had a good chat yesterday, and she wanted to discuss more wedding issues with Tasha this morning, which is why she's also looking for her."

Solomon and Linda looked curiously at Zivah.

"Let's return to Rose Cottage," Keya suggested, feigning cheerfulness.

Outside the garden gate, she hesitated. What if the cottage was a crime scene? But she was too late. Tasha's parents hurried up the path, calling Tasha's name.

"Go with them," she instructed Zivah. "Make them comfortable with tea and coffee but try to keep them in the living room and kitchen."

"Why?" asked Zivah slowly.

"Please, just do as I ask."

As Zivah entered Rose Cottage, Keya called Ryan.

"Have you been making jokes about the ghost?" asked Ryan when he answered.

"I thought it was rather witty."

"Nick doesn't think so. He's the one being accused of not taking the whole ghost thing seriously."

"Well, I'm more concerned about Tasha Nkosi's disappearance."

"Can we call it that?"

"There's still no sign of her at her cottage, and her parents are here now. Zivah and I have walked some of the river path and Zivah might also have looked round the village green. Ryan, why would she leave her phone?"

"That's a good point. What do you want to do?"

Keya hesitated. She didn't want to create a fuss. Not with all the reporters in the village. Tasha vanishing a week before her wedding would make the regional news headlines, and with the press presence, probably the national ones too. She needed to speak to Tasha's fiancé.

"I'll try to speak to Ezra Farmer, her fiancé. I think she was out with him and his parents last night. Maybe she never came home and is still with him."

"And her phone?"

"She forgot it?"

Ryan breathed deeply and exhaled, before asking, "Why are you so worried? Surely, most brides have second thoughts and act a bit absent-mindedly before their big day. And she's not a young, innocent girl. She'll know what she's doing."

Keya thought through Ryan's statement, before admitting, "I'm worried about her. And I feel responsible if something has happened."

"But why?"

"I've met her twice. And yesterday with Zivah, things were a bit … off. She isn't the excited bride-to-be, and it's not just second thoughts. I think she really loves her fiancé. It's everything else that's getting to her. I was so concerned I even gave her the contact details for the Samaritans in case she needed someone impartial to talk to. But what if she's done something stupid?"

"If she has, it isn't your fault. She's a grown adult and we have no jurisdiction in mental health cases. Only a doctor can recommend police intervention, via the courts. I'm sure you and Zivah spending time talking to her will have helped."

"Then where is she?" Keya cried.

"I'm coming over. Keep calm. And you're right. The first thing we need to do is contact her fiancé."

Keya felt helpless. Powerless.

Breathing deeply, she wandered back towards the river across the green until she heard Ryan call, "Keya."

He entered the cottage, but as she reached the garden gate, he stepped outside again. "Tasha's father gave me her fiancé's number. Zivah's doing a great job chatting away to him and his wife, but I can tell they're worried. Do you want to make the call, or shall I?"

Keya took a deep breath and stood taller. "I will."

A male voice answered her call.

"Is that Ezra Farmer?"

The voice replied hesitantly, "Who's calling?"

"Sergeant Keya Varma. I'm with Gloucestershire Police."

"What's happened? Is it Tasha?"

Keya hated that whenever she contacted someone, they presumed the worst. But then she rarely contacted people with good news.

"We're not aware of anything seriously wrong, but Tasha's cottage door was left open and there's no sign of her in the village. We wondered if she was still with you?"

"No. I dropped her back after supper with my parents last night. We thought it the right thing to do. I came home and I've been working all morning. I have called, but she didn't answer her phone."

"That's because she left it in the cottage. Do you know of anyone in Coln Akeman she might be visiting?"

"No. I know she went out with an old friend this week and she said an Indian girl and her police sister had called round and their chat had really helped. Oh, was that you?"

"Yes. And my sister Zivah. How was Tasha last night?"

"Distant. But then she's been like that for a while with my parents. I'm afraid they've rather taken over and are conducting our wedding like an orchestral symphony. If I'm honest, I've thought more than once about eloping and I know Tasha would prefer to get married on a Caribbean island, with just the two of us. But my parents would kill me, and I know Tasha's parents, particularly her father, are proud and overjoyed about our upcoming wedding."

None of this helped to find out where Tasha was now.

"I'm coming over," Ezra announced.

"Be careful of the press," warned Keya, but he'd already finished the call.

Keya looked at Ryan, shaking her head.

"It's only been a few hours. I'm sure she'll turn up," he comforted.

Keya caught movement behind Ryan and groaned.

The zealous female reporter was striding towards her. Was she returning to question Keya again about the ghost? She probably hadn't appreciated her joke.

Keya smiled to herself, but it froze on her face when the reporter called, "Is that where Tasha Nkosi is staying? Has something happened to her?"

CHAPTER FOURTEEN

As the female reporter approached Keya and Ryan, Keya whispered, "Get Nick," before she disappeared inside Rose Cottage, shutting the door behind her.

Zivah met her in the small hallway. "Thank goodness you're here, sis. I'm not sure what else to say or do with Tasha's parents."

"I'll go and tell them Ezra's on his way over."

"Did Ryan call him? Has he seen Tasha?"

"I called and no, he hasn't seen her since last night."

"This doesn't look good, does it?"

Keya wanted to be hopeful, and optimistic, but she had to admit, it did look as if Tasha Nkosi had deliberately disappeared, or worse ...

She shook her head, fixed her face into a professionally blank expression, and entered the living room.

"Mr and Mrs Nkosi. Your daughter's fiancé is on his way over." Keya saw that Linda was about to speak. "But I'm afraid he hasn't seen or spoken to your daughter since he dropped her back here last night. I'm going to have to call this in as a missing person case."

Linda gasped.

"That way," Keya reassured her, "we can use all our official resources to help find her."

Keya returned to the front door and opened it an inch. The coast was clear. She presumed the female reporter had followed Ryan. Feeling guilty that she might have subjected Ryan to the reporter's questions, she stepped into the garden and called Inspector Evans.

"Sergeant Varma, I wasn't expecting to hear from you. But if you're at a loose end, I'm sure your colleagues would appreciate your help again with the reporters and ghost-hunting public at Coln Akeman."

"I'm at Coln Akeman, sir. PC Jenkins contacted me this morning, concerned that a woman I visited yesterday had left her front door open and hadn't returned."

"What woman?"

"She's called Natasha Nkosi. And I propose opening a missing person case on her."

"Why? How long has she been gone?"

"Her fiancé dropped her back at the cottage she's renting last night, and nobody's seen her since. My sister and I have searched the river path, but there's no sign of her. And her parents are here now, and they haven't seen her either."

Keya paused and took a breath. "And, sir, she's a bit of a local celebrity as she's the poster girl for Farmers Jewellers, and due to marry their son a week today. One reporter is already sniffing around. With the lack of ghost sightings at the moment, this case could blow up."

"Then it's a good job we have our newly trained press liaison specialist, Sergeant Unwin, there."

"Will you come over?" Keya asked.

"No," replied Inspector Evans. "My presence will only fan the flames. Besides, after recent events with other forces, I have to ensure the paperwork for this case is meticulous. If it all goes wrong, and the worst happens, we'll have the press and the police authorities scrutinising our every move. We can't afford to make any mistakes."

Keya gulped, already feeling the weight of the case on her shoulders.

"I need you to obtain her personal details, age, address, contact information etc, and then start piecing together her last movements. Her parents should be able to help with that. And find her fiancé."

"I've already done that, sir. He's coming over."

"Good. Interview him and find out what he knows about her recent movements, and where she might go, and," the Inspector hesitated, "her state of mind."

"That's why I'm worried, sir. I visited her yesterday, with my sister on a wedding-related matter, and I was concerned about her. We both gave her our numbers, and I handed her contact details for the Samaritans in case she needed to talk to a third party. Now I'm worried I should have done more."

"I'm sure there's nothing more you could have done, but I will need your written report from that meeting. Was that the first time you met her?"

"No, sir. I first visited her on Wednesday. You see, her wedding, next week, is at the same venue my sister's was supposed to be."

"Supposed to be?" queried the inspector.

"The venue made a mistake. We visited Miss Nkosi to see if she'd be willing to move the wedding, but she told us that was impossible as her in-laws had made all the arrangements. So Zivah, my sister, and I have spent the last couple of days trying to find an alternative venue and ..."

"Sergeant," interrupted the Inspector. "This all sounds complicated, and you'll need to include it in your report, but is it relevant to the case at hand?"

Keya took a deep breath. "No, sir. Except that I do have concerns for her mental well-being."

There was a tapping sound on the phone. Keya thought it was from the inspector's pencil drumming against his desk. "Stan Rowbottom's in. I'll see if he can help and start by contacting the local hospitals. Give me a description of Natasha Nkosi."

As Keya described Tasha to the inspector, she glanced up and saw Ryan and Nick striding down the path along the side of the green, followed by a pack of reporters.

"Sir, I have to go."

"Sergeant, you're the lead officer on this at the scene. You need to arrange further searches of the area, and door-to-door enquiries. If Miss Nkosi has left any computer or technical equipment, see if young Ryan can access it. And interview her parents and fiancé to try to piece together her movements yesterday and last night. And Sergeant Unwin can help when he's not preening in front of the press.

Mind you, I don't envy him his role if Miss Nkosi doesn't show up today."

"Yes, sir."

Keya finished the call as Sergeant Nick Unwin reached her. He was wearing a charcoal grey suit, rather than a police uniform, and was younger than Keya, in his late twenties. He wore his dark hair long on top, styled into a quiff, but his handsome face looked strained, with worry lines between his eyebrows.

"We need somewhere to speak in private, away from this crowd." He motioned behind him with his head to the gathering reporters. "And not in the cottage."

Ryan joined them and nodded in agreement.

Keya confirmed, "I know. It might be a crime scene, which is why I've asked Zivah to keep Tasha's parents in the living room and kitchen, but she can't stop them moving around the cottage."

"Zivah?" queried Nick.

"My sister. She was with me when Ryan called, and she got on well with Tasha when we visited yesterday."

"I'm not sure she can continue to be involved. Not if we make this official," Nick commented.

"I just have. That was the inspector on the phone. He made it clear that we have to tread carefully and be meticulous in handling this case. Especially if it becomes a news story."

"Which it will," confirmed Nick.

Keya looked at Ryan. "You have the most to do. You need to search the area near the cottage, speaking to Tasha's neighbours and trying to access her phone. And we need to give you space and draw the reporters away."

Keya paused. She needed somewhere away from the cottage to conduct interviews. There was the pub, or Dr Peter's surgery, but both of them would be busy today. And if they needed to speak to the press, they'd need somewhere bigger. Gilly Wimsey. That was it.

"I think we should move our command centre …"

Nick raised his eyebrows. Was that too grand a name for it?

"To Akemans. It's outside the village, so it'll draw some reporters away and give Ryan space for his enquiries." She looked at Ryan. "I'm sure Zivah will help, as she's really worried about Tasha, and she'll be able to speak to Tasha if and when you find her. But we can't involve her officially, of course."

"Actually, Akeman's is an excellent idea," agreed Nick. "If we commandeer the auction house, I can use it for press conferences and meetings with leading members of the community."

Keya nodded her head. If they didn't locate Tasha within the next few hours, they'd need to speak to leading community members to inform them what was happening, in the unlikely event they hadn't already heard on the news, and ask for their assistance.

Although, as lead investigator, she should conduct the meetings, if Nick was happy to do so, she might leave them to him.

"And it's somewhere we can interview Tasha's family. As well as looking for Tasha, the inspector wants us to account for her movements since Zivah and I visited her yesterday morning."

"Akemans it is," announced Nick.

And Keya's first case as lead investigating officer.

"I'll call Ezra Farmer and ask him to meet us there," said Keya. "And Nick, can you drive Tasha's parents? I'm not sure my little Polo is appropriate." She looked at Ryan and Nick and asked, "Any questions?"

They both shook their heads.

"Let's find Tasha."

CHAPTER FIFTEEN

As Keya finished speaking to Nick and Ryan, a young man with copper coloured skin strode past the pack of reporters.

Some of them started whispering and when he opened the gate into the garden of Rose Cottage, Keya strode over and called, "Ezra Farmer."

The young man stopped, turned and frowned at her. "Are you speaking to me?"

"Yes. Are you Ezra Farmer?"

The young man laughed. "No, I'm Nate Nkosi. Tasha's brother." His face became serious, and he lowered his voice as he said, "My parents called me. We're all staying in the next village. They said Tasha's missing and asked me to come over."

"Tasha's brother?" Keya raised her eyebrows. Tasha had talked affectionately about her sister, but she hadn't mentioned a brother.

"Yes, now if you don't mind. I need to see my parents."

"Actually, Mr Nkosi. Do you have a car?"

"Yes." He narrowed his eyes at her, as if she'd asked a trick question.

"Then can you drive your parents to Akemans antiques centre, about a mile along the road towards Cirencester. We need to speak to you all about Tasha, but not here. Not with all these ..."

She turned towards the reporters who were peppering Nick with questions about Tasha.

Keya felt a sense of urgency. She needed to move the Nkosis to Akemans now. Before the reporters bore down on them.

She turned back to Nate. "And I need you all to go now." She strode down the path and opened the door. In the living room she said, "The press are outside and they know Tasha is missing. We need to get you out of here."

Solomon stood up but Linda protested, "What about Tasha? What if she comes back and we're not here?"

"PC Ryan is staying and so is Zivah." Keya looked across at her sister, who stared back at her, her mouth falling open in surprise. Keya gave her a quick nod before insisting, "We must go. Immediately. Nate is here and he'll drive you."

"But where are we going?"

"Somewhere quiet, but not far away." Keya escorted the Nkosis outside.

When Linda saw Nate, she threw her arms around him and started sobbing. Solomon held his head high, apparently unmoved by the drama unfolding around him.

"PC Jenkins," Keya called. "Please escort the Nkosis to their son's car."

The crowd of reporters still questioning Nick had swelled, and some of them must have realised what was happening as they broke away and approached Rose Cottage.

"Go," urged Keya, ushering the Nkosis out of the garden and onto the footpath beside the green.

Nate seemed about to stop and speak to the reporters, but Solomon grabbed his wife by the elbow and pulled her down the path. "Come, Nate," he called. "We do not want our business all over the papers."

Nate looked at the reporters and then the stony look on Ryan's face and decided to follow his parents.

Keya didn't realise she'd been holding her breath until she exhaled in relief. Nick extracted himself from the reporters and strode across the green towards The Axeman. Most of the reporters followed him, although some turned to stare at Keya. Time to leave.

She stepped back into Rose Cottage and dialled Ezra Farmer's number.

"Do you have news?" He asked, answering her call before she'd even heard a ringtone.

"I'm afraid not. But we are taking Tasha's disappearance seriously and it's now officially a missing person case. I'd like you to meet me at Akemans auction house, not Rose Cottage."

"Why?"

She could hardly tell him the cottage was a potential crime scene.

"Because of all the reporters in Coln Akeman. We'll have some privacy at the auction house. Nate Nkosi is driving his parents over there as we speak. And I'll meet you there shortly."

She finished the call before Ezra could protest or ask any more questions. Her next call was to Gilly Wimsey.

"Hi Keya. Have you seen the news about the ghost? The village is swamped with reporters."

"I know. Which is why I need to ask a favour. A woman's gone missing, and we need somewhere away from the press to interview her family. I've sent them to you. Can we use the auction house? I thought it would be quiet at the moment."

"Oh dear. You sound very serious. But of course you can use the auction house. I think Norman is still in, sorting out collections from the last auction, and storing items for this month. But George is out, so it's peaceful."

"Can you open the front door and turn the lights on? And meet the Nkosi family. It's their daughter who's missing. I'll be with you as soon as I can. Oh, and look out for Ezra Farmer."

"Of Farmers Jewellers? The one who's getting married next week?"

"Yes. If his bride turns up. She the one who's missing."

Keya finished the call as Gilly began oohing and aahing. She'd speak to her about the case later, but now she had other things to deal with.

She found Zivah in the kitchen washing up.

"Thank you, but you better leave those. Tasha is officially missing, which means the cottage is a potential crime scene."

Zivah gasped and stepped away from the sink as if the water had burnt her hands. "Poor Tasha."

Keya closed her eyes, trying to think. So much was happening and all at once. Opening her eyes and looking at her sister, she said, "I know I said I'd help find a marquee company, and sort out your wedding, but Inspector Evans has made me the lead officer on this case."

"We must find Tasha," exclaimed Zivah. "My wedding can wait. What do you need me to do?"

Relieved, Keya replied, "Help Ryan. We need to continue searching the village for Tasha, and speak to neighbours, and see if we can access her phone."

"I tried her phone, but it's password protected."

"I'll ask her fiancé if he knows what the code is. And I better go. I'm meeting him at Akemans. That's where we're going to base ourselves for the investigation. Are you OK staying here with Ryan? He has a car, but I suspect he'll be too busy to drive you anywhere for a while."

"I don't need to be anywhere. And I want to help. If you're still busy later, I'll call Aadi and ask him to collect me."

"OK."

Zivah stepped forward and hugged Keya. "You can do this. Find Tasha. She needs our help."

"I know."

Keya left Rose Cottage and met Ryan on the path outside.

He told her, "The Nkosis are on their way to Akemans."

"Thanks. Zivah's still inside. She says she can't open Tasha's phone. I'll see if anyone knows her password, so for now can you and Zivah start searching the village? And see if there's a spare key to lock the house. I don't want any reporters, or worse still, digital detectives wandering in."

Keya left Ryan and walked towards her parked car.

"Where's Natasha Nkosi?" shouted a male voice.

"Do you suspect foul play?" shouted another.

Keya held her head up high, ignoring the questions.

"Do you suspect Ezra Farmer of killing his fiancé? Did he know about her pregnancy?"

Keya froze, but then urged herself to walk on.

She unlocked her car and climbed inside. Fumbling with her car keys, she started the car and drove forward, careful not to knock over an errant cameraman filming her departure.

Her hands shook.

Was Tasha pregnant?

CHAPTER SIXTEEN

Keya pulled into the gravel parking area in front of Akemans antiques centre and turned off her car engine. She sat for a minute, breathing deeply, and trying to clear her mind.

Then she placed her hands back on the steering wheel.

Her immediate thought was how had someone known Tasha was pregnant, or was the reporter fishing by throwing the question at her?

She didn't think Tasha was the innocent young woman her father had made her out to be, and she presumed, if Tasha was pregnant, that Ezra was the father. But if he wasn't? That opened a whole different line of enquiry.

She rang Inspector Evans.

"Have you found her?" he asked, his voice soft and full of concern.

She'd worked for Inspector Evans for six years, ignoring the short time she'd spent in the Rural, Heritage and Wildlife Unit, but she still didn't totally understand him.

Often grumpy, he had a tendency to bark orders and upset the junior staff in the police station, but he also had a caring, human side to his nature. And he was loyal and protective of his team, perhaps with the exception of Nick.

Keya suspected the inspector thought Nick had made a grave error of judgement in pursuing Dotty as a culprit rather than using her as an ally to help solve a series of murders and antique frauds.

"Sergeant. Are you there?"

"Yes, sorry, sir. I just thought you ought to know. As I was leaving Coln Akeman a reporter shouted at me asking about Tasha Nkosi's pregnancy."

"A pregnant missing bride," groaned the inspector.

"If she is. Nobody has mentioned it to me, including Tasha. But I thought you ought to know, and wondered if there was any way you could verify it?"

"We need her doctor's consent to do that. You get on with Dr Peter, don't you?"

"Yes," Keya replied hesitantly.

"Can you speak to him in case Miss Nkosi visited his surgery? And if she didn't, see if her parents know which doctor she's registered with."

"Yes, sir." Keya finished the call and found Dr Peter Wimsey's number.

The call must have been diverted as a woman answered. "Akeman Surgery. How can I help you?"

"This is Sergeant Varma. Is Dr Peter free?"

"I'm afraid he's with a patient. We're rather behind with this morning's surgery. Half the village is here," confided the receptionist. "I think they're either hiding from the press or wanting to catch up with the gossip."

Keya thought quickly. "I know you can't divulge medical information over the phone, but are you able to tell me if Natasha Nkosi registered with you as a temporary patient?"

"Let's have a look. Do you have her date of birth?"

"I'm afraid not."

"Address?"

"She was living in Rose Cottage, in the village."

Keya heard tapping keys.

"No, sorry, she didn't register with us."

"Thank you," said Keya.

"Do you still need Dr Peter to call you back?"

"No, you've told me what I needed to know. Thanks."

Keya finished the call and climbed out of her car. As she did so, a smart black SUV pulled into the car park, and she noticed a young man with short red hair and a goatee beard climb out.

The man called, "Sergeant Varma."

Keya stopped and waited for the man to walk across the gravel and join her.

"I'm Ezra Farmer. Any news on Tasha?"

Ezra was casually but expensively dressed, with brown shoes, cotton trousers, and a blue t-shirt and blazer. It struck her that he wasn't that tall. Perhaps not as tall as Tasha.

"I'm afraid not, Mr Farmer."

"Please call me Ezra, or I'll think you want to speak to my father. And can we talk here, before we meet Tasha's parents?"

Keya smiled apologetically. "I'd rather speak to you and her family together. Time is important and we don't want to waste any. I hope you understand."

"Of course." He nodded and followed Keya into the reception-cum-office area at Akemans.

As she always did, Keya glanced towards the antique, green leather-topped desk facing the door, hoping to see Dotty. But the desk was empty.

Tasha's parents were sitting on the grey sofa in the right-hand corner of the room and Nate was sitting opposite them, on a grey tub chair. Mugs of hot drinks were on the wooden coffee table between them.

Gilly bustled out of the office area behind the reception desk and asked, "Any news?"

Keya shook her head before introducing Ezra. "This is Tasha's fiancé, Ezra." She turned to Ezra. "Gilly runs the antiques centre next door and has kindly let us use the auction house as our base."

"Ezra, coffee?" asked Gilly.

"Yes, please."

Linda Nkosi saw Ezra and lifted a hand in greeting.

"Mr Farmer," said Keya.

He tilted his head as he looked at her.

"Ezra. Would you like to join Tasha's family?"

Keya rolled a spare office chair across the reception area as Gilly placed a cup of coffee in front of Ezra and another on the table.

"I thought you'd need something," Gilly said to Keya.

"Thanks. Where's Nick?" Keya asked.

"In the auction room, on his phone.

Keya pushed the chair into the gap, avoiding the table as it was covered with mugs. Instead, the chair bumped against the wall several times as she manoeuvred it into place.

She sat down, her cheeks burning. Not the professional start she'd wanted.

Ezra looked at her sincerely and said, "Thank you, Sergeant, for reacting so quickly. I always thought you had to wait twenty-four or forty-eight hours to report a missing person."

Keya smiled. "That's an urban myth. We take missing person cases very seriously, especially when we're concerned about their state of mind."

"State of mind?" queried Nate. "There's nothing wrong with Tasha. Are you saying she was mental or something?"

Keya flinched at his choice of words.

"I'm saying that when I visited Tasha yesterday, and the day before, she seemed anxious, even depressed."

"The wedding was getting to her," agreed Ezra in a low voice.

"Nonsense," countered Solomon. "My daughter is strong, like a cheetah. And she was looking forward to her wedding."

Linda placed her hand on her husband's thigh and said, "Solomon, she was rather quiet yesterday."

"And so she should be. This is a big step. An exciting one. Marrying this fine young man." Solomon raised his hand and gestured towards Ezra.

"Of course," Keya agreed. "Now, to help find Tasha, we need to piece together her movements over the past twenty-four hours. Zivah and I visited her yesterday, in the late morning. When we left, she said she was tired and that she was going to rest before you arrived, Mr and Mrs Nkosi. I don't think she'd been sleeping well. When did you get to her cottage?"

Solomon answered. "Regrettably, we were later leaving London than I'd arranged," he glanced at his son, "but we arrived at Coln Akeman at half past one."

"I'd brought lunch, so we sat down with Tasha to eat it," added Linda.

"And did she eat much?" asked Keya.

Solomon puffed out his chest, but Linda must have realised he was about to respond in defence of his daughter, so she said quickly, "No. She didn't have the best of appetites. Not like she did when she was a girl and always running around. I think it was the modelling world. All those painfully thin girls. It's not natural."

Keya agreed and smiled at Linda, who looked as if she enjoyed her food, and Keya could imagine her cooking hearty meals for her family.

"Did you arrive with your parents?" Keya asked Nate.

"Yes, we drove down together. And if you want my opinion, there's nothing wrong with Tasha. Sure, she played around with her food, but that wasn't unusual."

"But surely she needed to keep her strength up?" said Keya.

"Why?" Nate bristled.

Keya couldn't say 'because she might have been eating for two,' so instead she said, "Because of the wedding. It's a stressful time."

"It certainly is," Ezra agreed. "And I'll add that Tasha ordered a salad last night and still left half of it."

"Thank you," said Keya, before returning her attention to Linda. "How long did you stay with Tasha yesterday? Did you all go for a walk?"

Linda glanced at Nate before replying, "No. We were planning to do that this morning."

Really, after they'd walked all the way from the next village? Keya still didn't class them as the walking type.

Linda continued, "We left at half past three and agreed to see Tasha again this morning."

Keya remembered something Zivah had said and asked, "Did you stock the fridge for her?"

"I did bring some food, yes. I knew how bad she was at food shopping."

And there wasn't much choice in Coln Akeman. So how did Tasha buy provisions?

Keya groaned. She hadn't thought to look for a car. What if Tasha had driven to a friend's house? And she'd left her phone by mistake, or because she just needed a few days away from the drama of her wedding. Had she, Keya, started what the press were likely to blow up into a large-scale manhunt for nothing?

"Does Tasha have a car?" she asked,

"Yes," Ezra replied. "A black Audi A4."

CHAPTER SEVENTEEN

Outside Akemans auction house, Keya took a deep breath before phoning Ryan.

"Do you want an update?" asked Ryan when he answered.

"Only if you have something new to tell me."

"No, I'm afraid not."

"Look, I've been really stupid and overlooked Tasha having a car. She might just have driven to a friend's, or gone somewhere for a day to, I don't know, shop or explore the Cotswolds."

"Zivah found her car keys by the back door with a set for the cottage. And we found her Audi parked in the lane behind."

Keya didn't know whether to feel disappointed that Tasha hadn't gone out for the day or relieved that she wasn't wasting everyone's time, and the police's resources.

Returning to Tasha's family in the reception area, she said, "My colleagues have found Tasha's car parked behind Rose Cottage."

Ezra's shoulders drooped, and he said in a monotone voice, "I was hoping she'd gone shopping to Cheltenham or Oxford."

Linda gave him a motherly look.

Keya looked from Linda to Solomon and asked, "Why didn't you stay longer with Tasha yesterday? After all, you'd driven all the way down from London to see her." She stopped, realising that her personal feelings were getting in the way of the calm, professional demeanour she needed to maintain.

There was an uncomfortable silence.

Solomon and Linda both turned to stare at their son.

Nate shifted in his seat, and then admitted, "Because I needed the car to visit a backer for my new business."

"Oh, what are you doing?" Keya sat back and admonished herself. She was losing her professional cool.

"Battery recycling."

Keya composed herself and said, "That's a good idea. But I presume you need a lot of money to start the business."

"No, not really," Nate replied. "Especially as I have someone willing to provide the majority of the start-up capital."

"And is that who you visited yesterday?"

"Yes, I drove my parents back to our hotel in Coln St. Aldwyns and left for my meeting. I was back just after six."

Keya looked from Nate, to Linda, to Solomon, and asked, "Have any of you spoken to Tasha since you left her yesterday afternoon?"

They shook their heads.

"We tried to call this morning, but she didn't answer her phone," Solomon said.

Keya looked up at Ezra and asked, "I presume you picked Tasha up last night?"

"Yes. And we left Coln Akeman just after six to have supper with my parents at The Falcon in Cirencester."

"And how was she?"

"Withdrawn, but she'd become like that whenever my parents launched into the details of the wedding. They've completely taken over. I think Tasha was grateful at first, but then they started rejecting all her suggestions and eventually took over. After that, she gradually retreated from the whole event. And she lost some of her sparkle. I hoped that once the formalities were over, she'd return to her normal self."

"Did you say anything to your parents? Ask them to take a step back? To let you and Tasha organise the wedding?" asked Keya.

Ezra rubbed his chin and in an uncertain voice asked, "Why would I do that?"

Keya looked at him. He was being completely serious. It appeared that his parents organising his life, even his wedding, seemed natural to him.

Keya thought of her sister's wedding. Her mother had tried to take control of that but, frustrated, Zivah had sat down with her parents and told them she was happy for their input, and for their guidance on traditions, but it was her and Aadi's wedding, not theirs.

Mind you, Keya wasn't sure Aadi's parents had been quite so accommodating, especially in respect of the guest list. The wedding was much larger than Zivah had wanted. And how would they feel about a marquee rather than a hotel reception? But that would have to wait.

"So you, Tasha, and your parents all had supper together last night, and apart from Tasha being quiet, there were no disagreements or cross words?"

Ezra blinked before replying, "No. None."

"And what time did you drop Tasha at the cottage?"

"Just after eleven thirty. Then I drove back to my place and went to bed."

"And this morning?"

"I was working at home on the costings for a new branch, so I was in until you contacted me, apart from an early morning run to clear my head."

"And you haven't spoken to Tasha since you dropped her off?"

"No. I did try, but she didn't answer my call."

Keya picked up her mug and sipped her now cold coffee.

What she couldn't quite understand was why Tasha was down in the Cotswolds, living alone in a cottage, just weeks before her wedding. Surely she should be sharing the occasion with her friends. Enjoying the excitement of her upcoming big day.

But perhaps London and the wedding were too much, and she'd needed time out. Keya could imagine that many people living in the hustle and bustle of the capital city would see staying in a picturesque cottage in the Cotswolds as the perfect place to unwind and relax.

Uncertain of Tasha's reason's Keya asked, "Why was Tasha staying in Rose Cottage? How long has she been here?"

"She left London just over three weeks ago," Solomon announced.

An uncomfortable silence followed his statement.

"Why?" Keya pressed, drawing out the word.

"She needed some time to herself before the wedding," Linda said.

Which, Keya considered, was a bland response. There was something else. A reason that none of them were giving her.

Solomon continued, "My daughter needed to reflect on her life, in order to prepare for her future. To go forward with a clear head and a pure heart. And now we need to stop wasting time and concentrate on finding her."

Keya leaned forward and asked Solomon, "What do you think has happened to her?"

"Either she has gone for a long walk of self-contemplation, or someone has kidnapped her. I don't have much money, but Ezra's family does. Their money, combined with my daughter's beauty and grace, is a perfect target for some madman."

For the first time, Solomon's composure showed signs of crumbling. His hands tightened into fists as he fought to control himself. But Keya knew from the glistening in his eyes that he was close to tears.

Keya suddenly felt respect for this proud man.

She addressed the group. "Before we take a break, I need two pieces of information. Firstly, do any of you know the passcode for her phone?"

Everyone shook their heads.

"She used her thumb to open it. I've seen her," Linda said.

"Yes, but she'd have a backup code, too."

"Oh, I don't know what that was." Linda shook her head.

"OK. What about her doctor?" asked Keya. "Do you know which surgery she was registered with?"

"Of course. We all use the same doctor. We always have," Solomon replied.

"It's the Lavington Road Practice in Ealing. Dr Hassan," Linda confirmed.

Keya jotted the details down in her notebook.

"Thank you." Keya wheeled her chair into the corner of the room, so she had space to stand up.

As she walked out of the reception into the car park, she sensed someone following her. She stopped, turned around, and came face-to-face with Nate.

"I know I shouldn't, but I do know Tasha's phone passcode. I've watched her tap it in."

Keya kept her face impassive. Who was she to judge Nate? Especially since he was offering vital information that could help locate his sister. "Go on," she encouraged.

"77977."

Keya repeated, "77977. Thank you. I'll tell my colleague."

Keya waited, watching Nate return to the reception area. Then she called Ryan.

"Hi, Keya. Did Tasha's fiancé say anything about a row?"

"No, why?"

"I interviewed the man who lives next door again."

Keya remembered the elderly gentleman and the snippets of conversations she'd heard, including the words 'visitors' and 'young men'.

"And he said he heard Tasha and a man shouting last night. Twice. First at around half past five ..."

Which might have been when Ezra picked Tasha up.

"And again, much later. He thinks around half past eleven. It woke him up."

Ezra had told her he'd dropped Tasha off at half past eleven.

"Why didn't he tell you this earlier?" Keya asked.

"Said he didn't like to interfere in other people's business, but he'd heard on the radio we were looking for Tasha, so he thought he'd better tell us."

Keya sighed. Members of the public could be a great help if they opened up. Then she thought of the digital detectives and the ghost hunters. As long as they weren't motivated by self-interest and trying to be famous.

"Thank you. I'll speak to Ezra about that. But I'm calling because Tasha's brother thinks he knows the password for her phone."

"Just a minute," Ryan replied.

Keya waited.

"I've got the phone. Go ahead."

"77977," said Keya, and then she heard tapping.

"Bingo. We're in," announced Ryan, excitedly.

"What can you see?"

"Loads of missed calls. The phone log has several from Ezra this morning and also from her dad. And she called her mum at a quarter to six last night."

"I wonder if she needed to speak to her after her row with Ezra?"

"Let's see what else there is."

Keya waited again.

"This is interesting. She had a text conversation with someone called Dan late last night. And in the last one he says he'll come over. Do you think that's the same Dan she was at The Axeman with?"

"My fit-out contractor!" Keya exclaimed.

CHAPTER EIGHTEEN

Keya was about to return to the reception area when Nick walked out. She'd forgotten he was in the auction room.

"How did you get on with the family?" Nick asked. "Any leads?"

"Afraid not, but Ryan's heard from a neighbour that Tasha and a young man were shouting at each other yesterday."

"The fiancé?"

"I presume so. I'm going to speak to him again. What about you?"

"Stan's called all the hospitals in the area, but nobody fitting Miss Nkosi's description has been admitted. And I've contacted local shelters and received the same response. Ryan said her car was still there, so I phoned around the local car rental agencies but drew a blank. Stan suggested speaking to the local bus operator. Although the buses are infrequent through Coln Akeman, there was one at quarter past seven this morning going to Cirencester."

Keya hadn't thought of all these possibilities, as she'd been so concerned with physically looking for Tasha and speaking to her family.

"And I've also been tracking the news," Nick added, "and the story of Miss Nkosi's disappearance has broken."

"Do you want to hold a press conference?"

"Yes, but first I suggest we speak to the locals and engage their help."

"Good idea. Who were you thinking of?"

"I thought you might have some suggestions as the Rural Engagement Officer."

Keya thought of influential people in the village, and the local area.

"There's Dr Peter Wimsey to start with. As the local doctor people confide in him. But Tasha didn't. I've already checked. And then there's the vicar. Coln Akeman is part of a larger parish, and the vicarage is a not particularly attractive brick bungalow in Coln St Aldwyns. The Church of England sold the lovely old vicarage because it couldn't afford to heat or repair it ..."

"Anyone else?" Nick cut in.

"The landlord from The Axeman, the lady who runs the Post Office, and the owner of the village shop. They meet most of the locals and some of the visitors to the area. Then there's the parish council, the WI, the local primary school. Oh, and Gilly Wimsey. She knows most people, and as we're basing ourselves here, it would be sensible to involve her."

"OK, I'll phone round. It's half past twelve now. Shall we aim for a meeting here in two hours? That should give me time to contact everyone."

"Yes, and I need to organise some food," said Keya. "I don't know about you, but I'm starving. I was called out before I had time for breakfast."

"If only there was a cafe at Akemans we could visit." Nick grinned at Keya and she rolled her eyes.

"At this rate, I'm never going to open it."

Keya returned to Tasha's family and said, "We all need to eat. But I should warn you that Tasha's disappearance has made the news, which is not surprising with all the reporters hanging around Coln Akeman."

"Tasha told us they were interested in a ghost," Solomon remarked.

"Yes, one they've named the Weeping Widow, although I doubt anyone has heard her cry and I'm certain nobody knows her marital status. If she exists at all."

"I saw footage, and it was pretty convincing," Nate said.

"So perhaps we could have something delivered?" suggested Ezra.

"We're too far from anywhere, I'm afraid. There is a farm shop on the way to Cirencester. I could go and buy us all some sandwiches."

Solomon shook his head. "You are a police officer, not a delivery person. Nate will go, and I will pay."

Solomon fixed his eyes on Nate, who looked about to protest, before he nodded in acceptance.

"Any special requests?" asked Nate.

"I'm a vegetarian," Keya responded.

"So that's one vegetarian and everyone else can pick from whatever selection I find. See you in a bit." Nate pulled a set of car keys out of his pocket and walked out of the reception area.

"Despite our earlier walk, I need some fresh air," Solomon said, standing up.

"We'll come with you," Ezra suggested, as he also stood up.

As Linda pulled herself to her feet, Keya said, "Actually, Ezra, may I speak to you again?"

Solomon, who was halfway across the reception area, stopped.

"Don't worry, Mr Nkosi, there's nothing to worry about. But I do need to speak to your future son-in-law in private." Keya hoped she was right, and that there was nothing sinister about the row that Tasha's neighbour had overheard.

When the door closed behind Linda and Solomon, Keya sat down on the grey sofa.

"My colleague talked to Tasha's neighbours," she began, "and one of them heard shouting yesterday. What did you argue about?"

Ezra sat back down on a tub chair. "Argue? We didn't, but that would make sense. Was the row sometime before six? Only Tasha was speaking to her mum when I arrived, and I heard her say something about being put under pressure, and it wasn't fair. It was her life. But when I asked her about it, she said it was nothing and clammed up."

"Did she tell you, or did you overhear her say who was pressuring her?"

Ezra pursed his lips and shook his head. "Sorry, I don't."

"But what about when you returned from supper? Did you have a disagreement then?"

"No. Tasha said she was tired and wanted to go to bed. I'd have liked to stay with her longer, but she insisted I leave, so I did."

Keya thought Ezra was telling the truth, but if he was, who else would Tash meet so late at night? It didn't make sense.

"Did you see anyone when you left the cottage, or notice anything unusual?"

Ezra paused and looked towards the auction room door as he thought.

Keya could hear a murmur from the other side. It must be Nick arranging the community meeting.

"There was a car whose lights switched off when I approached, but I presumed it was someone from the pub."

If the person was leaving the pub, they'd turn their car lights on, Keya thought.

"Did you notice anything about the car?"

"Not really. I had the impression it was big, but not like an SUV or 4x4. The type of car a salesman would drive, needing comfort and speed on long journeys. But I can't tell you why that thought popped into my head. Maybe because I was thinking of the new shop we're planning to open in Leamington Spa. It's some distance from our current shops and if I'm managing it, I'll have a lot of driving to do."

The door from the auction room opened and Nick walked in.

"We haven't formally met," he said to Ezra, who stood up.

"Sergeant Nick Unwin. I'll be dealing with the press and outside agencies on this case."

"Glad to have you on the team, and thank you for your help so far. I'm Ezra Farmer."

"Ezra, we've holding a meeting with members of the local community in an hour and a half. You're welcome to join us. In fact, I hope you will, but I'd rather your future parents-in-law didn't. Any idea how we handle them?"

"You could suggest they return to their hotel, but Solomon is a proud man. It's his Zulu heritage. He won't want to leave while his daughter is in trouble. But next door is an antiques centre, isn't it?"

"Yes," replied Keya.

"Then perhaps we could persuade Linda to take him round that while we have the meeting. And to appease him, you could suggest he and Linda join us at the end so we can update them with any progress or plan of action."

"That's an excellent suggestion," agreed Nick.

Keya looked from him to Ezra. It certainly was. And she was beginning to feel out of her depth with this case. She didn't mind organising searches and interviewing people, but strategy and politics, even just family ones, weren't her strength.

The front door opened, and Linda and Solomon stepped inside, followed by Nate carrying several brown paper bags. "Lunch time," he announced.

CHAPTER NINETEEN

Keya ate her sandwiches quickly, and then went to the antiques centre, searching for Gilly Wimsey.

"Come in," Gilly said, when Keya found her in her first-floor office. "And find a space to sit down."

That was easier said than done. Piles of papers and boxes rested on the three spare wooden chairs. Keya removed one of the boxes, which had table lamps sticking out of the top of it, and placed it on the equally messy floor.

"I do miss Dotty," sighed Gilly. "She made sure I kept this place tidy, and her stall on the first floor was an excellent place to sell unwanted stock at discount prices."

"I thought you'd keep that going."

"I'm trying to, but with the antiques centre, extra work in the auction house, and the cafe construction work, I just don't have the time." Gilly sat back in her chair and closed her eyes.

"What about finding a replacement for Dotty?"

"I have tried, but it's surprisingly difficult. Nobody wants to be flexible. Receptionists only want to sit at the front desk and answer calls, and office managers refuse to work as receptionists. But that's not how we work here, as you know. Everyone has to muck in when and where they're needed. Anyway, that's enough of my woes. What about this missing girl?"

Keya wasn't sure Tasha classified as a girl, but she supposed her demeanour yesterday had been like that of a lost child. Was that only yesterday? But back to today.

"There's a meeting in," Keya checked her watch, "forty-five minutes to update and engage members of the local community. Nick has invited Dr Peter, and I thought you might like to join us."

"Oh yes," and then perhaps because she didn't want to sound too enthusiastic, Gilly added in a serious tone, "I'd like to help. Where are you holding the meeting?"

"In the auction room?"

"Then we'll need to set out chairs. Luckily, I bought a set of stacking office ones which nobody wanted at the last auction. They should still be in the main auction room. I'll ask Norman to arrange them, and to fetch some of the cafe chairs from the storeroom."

Keya stood up. "Thanks. I better go and check on Tasha's family, but I'll see you later."

As Keya descended the metal staircase, her phone rang. She hurried down the rest of the stairs before answering the call.

"Yes, sir," she said a little breathlessly.

"Have you been running?" asked Inspector Evans.

"Not exactly. But I am helping Sergeant Unwin prepare for the community meeting."

Inspector Evans cleared his throat. "I wanted to talk to you about that. I'm sorry, but with the press coverage, the case has reached divisional level. And they've insisted on sending a specialist team to organise the search and take over the investigation. They'll be with you for that meeting. They indicated that as you're close to the family, they'd like you to continue working with them, although they're also bringing in a specially trained family liaison officer. I'm sorry. I gave you control of the case, but now you'll have to hand it over to Chief Inspector Greg."

Keya allowed the inspector's words to sink in. And as she did, she felt a release of pressure in her mind.

"Actually, Inspector. That's a relief. I've realised I can't be strategic about the investigation when I'm so closely associated with Tasha, and now her family. But I do feel responsible for her disappearance."

"Sergeant, listen to me," growled the inspector. "Whatever happens, you are not accountable for Miss Nkosi's actions. You offered your help, and whether she decided to take your advice or not is up to her."

"Yes, sir." Keya knew he was right, but it didn't change how she felt.

"At this meeting, the new team will ask for volunteers for a full-scale search of the local area. But I have my concerns, especially with the River Coln being so close. Too easy for a victim to fall in, accidentally or deliberately, and it can be days or weeks before the body is discovered. So, while the team from Gloucester pursues the missing person hypothesis, I want you to look at it from the angle that Miss Nkosi is dead."

Keya gasped.

"I know, and let's hope I'm wrong, but that's not what my gut is telling me. So if her body does turn up, I want us to have gathered as much evidence as possible and be ahead of the game. Does that make sense?"

"Yes, sir."

"I don't have to tell you that the next twenty-four hours are critical to finding Miss Nkosi alive, so do what you feel is necessary to help, but remember my orders."

Keya said a final, "Yes, sir," before finishing the call.

She looked around the large internal mill space which housed the antiques centre. Rows of booths stretched back to the new partition wall, which separated the centre from Keya's café space.

Mirrors, pictures, and vintage signs, including a prominent yellow and red one advertising Shell motor oil, were displayed on the whitewashed walls.

As she became aware of her surroundings, she heard the hum of voices, the odd cough, and the laugh of a nearby stall holder. Members of the public ambled past. It felt safe in here.

If she fell over, or had a fit, she knew someone would come to her rescue and call a doctor or ambulance. But what about Tasha? Was she lying somewhere injured and in pain?

Keya wanted to help. Physically help. Not sit at a desk directing others. That wasn't her style.

She watched Gilly enter the auction house, took a deep breath, and followed her.

Time for the next stage of the investigation.

CHAPTER TWENTY

Keya returned to the reception area of the Akemans auction room. Ezra and Tasha's family were finishing their lunch. Solomon wiped his hands on a white paper napkin and stood up.

"Any news?" he asked.

Keya reached the spare office chair at the end of the table and said, "I've just been informed that a specialist team from Gloucester will arrive shortly to take over the investigation."

Linda's eyes widened in alarm. She said in a worried tone, "But we like you. You met Tasha. You understand."

"And I'm still helping to find her. But our station has limited resources and I'm the Cotswold's Rural Engagement Officer. I don't have the specialist skills to find a missing person that this team has. But if you have any concerns, please bring them to me. You will be assigned a trained family liaison officer, but I'm here if you need me."

Ezra turned to her. "That does sound sensible, although it also highlights the seriousness of Tasha's disappearance. But I'm certainly grateful for all you, the police, are doing."

The auction room door opened, and Gilly poked her head round it. "Can I borrow you?"

"Excuse me," Keya said and followed Gilly.

Norman was standing by a stack of metal chairs with black fabric covers.

"Where would you like these?" Gilly asked.

"I'd say in rows facing the raised platform where your sister sits when running auctions."

Norman removed the top chair and placed it on the ground. As he continued his unstacking, Keya and Gilly moved the chairs into two short rows.

"A team from Gloucester is taking over," said Keya.

"That must be who contacted Nick. He rushed out, saying something about meeting a new team. I hope they're not too demanding."

Keya looked round the auction room space. "They'll need tables, and somewhere to sit. These office chairs will be ideal, and we could use the cafe tables."

Gilly turned to Norman. "Did you hear that? We have to prepare the auction room for another police team. So can you bring more chairs, and also fetch some tables?"

"I hope they're not expecting state-of-the-art equipment," grumbled Norman.

"I'm sure they're used to working in village halls and community buildings," Keya replied. But were they? Would they start ordering Norman, Gilly, and even her around to bring them this or that, or to make drinks?

Dr Peter walked into the auction room. "Terrible business. Just awful." He shook his head. When he reached Keya, he said, "You called the surgery. Sorry we couldn't be more help, but Tasha Nkosi didn't register with us, even temporarily."

Keya remembered she had the details of Tasha's doctor's surgery. She should call them as she didn't want the new team discovering Tasha was pregnant, and thinking badly of her, or telling the press about it without considering the implications.

"Excuse me," she said and left Dr Peter and Gilly arranging more chairs which Norman had brought from the storeroom.

She entered a second, smaller room used to display pictures and individual household items for an auction. Taking out her notebook, she placed it on a glass display cabinet, usually filled with jewellery and silver items.

She looked up the contact number for the Lavington Road Practice in Ealing and then phoned them. Her call was answered by a male receptionist.

"Hi, my name is Sergeant Keya Varma and I'm calling from the village of Coln Akeman in the Cotswolds."

The receptionist exclaimed. "Oh, my! I've just been watching the news. That's where Natasha Nkosi has disappeared."

Relieved to have an opening in the conversation, Keya said. "It is and we're doing our best to find her. I've been tasked with looking into her mental and physical health history." Which wasn't exactly true, but she continued, "And I believe Natasha is a patient at your surgery."

"She was, up until two months ago." The receptionist lowered his voice. "There was rather a nasty scene in Dr Hassan's office which spilled over into the reception area. Miss Nkosi accused him of telling her family private medical details." He paused. Dramatically.

"Really," said Keya, playing along.

"I know. That's a serious allegation, but not actually that uncommon in the community round here. Parents want to know everything about their children's medical conditions, even when they're grown adults."

Keya thought of her Indian community and understood the sentiment, although families were becoming more accepting of each other's privacy.

"So what happened?" Keya asked.

"Miss Nkosi said she'd find another doctor, and she did. I processed the request for her medical records from the … Just a minute. Let me find the details."

Keya heard keys tapping.

"Here we are. The Elizabeth Blackwell Clinic in Kensington."

Keya thought that sounded like an upmarket medical practice. She asked, "Is that private?"

"No, but it is exclusively for women, and women's issues."

Like pregnancy, thought Keya.

"Would you like their telephone number?" asked the receptionist.

"Yes, please." Keya wrote the number down. "Thank you for your help."

"Not at all," squeaked the receptionist. "I can't wait to tell my friends I've been questioned and provided useful information in the Tasha Nkosi disappearance."

Keya realised her questions could make other people wonder why she was asking them, so she said, "Although you won't tell anybody how you helped, will you? This is a crucial time in the investigation and medical information is, as you know, confidential."

The details of a patient's medical practice weren't, but she wanted to make sure the receptionist kept quiet.

"Of course. Mum's the word."

Keya finished the call and heard unfamiliar voices in the main auction room. One of them was a man's, and he was barking out orders. She hoped he didn't annoy Norman, who'd complain to Aunt Beanie, and also to Ryan, who was currently living in a cottage at Meadowbank Farm.

She needed to update Ryan, but first she wanted to call The Elizabeth Blackwell Clinic.

"Good afternoon," said a well-spoken young woman.

Keya introduced herself again and said, "I understand Natasha Nkosi recently registered with you."

"That's correct. Miss Nkosi is a patient, but I can't give out any medical information. You'll need to email your request using the national police NHS number."

Keya wasn't aware of such a number, but it made sense. Rather than doctors and police arguing about releasing information, a number, like a secret code, would allow the police access to sensitive records.

"What email address should I use?"

Keya wrote down the one the woman gave her.

"Thank you."

Keya returned to the auction room, which was filling up with people. She recognised the elderly vicar, two members of the Women's Institute, and the landlord of The Axeman.

As she walked towards the group gathered round the rows of chairs, a man in a dark suit with a shaven head stepped forward.

"Sergeant Varma?"

"Yes."

"I'm Chief Inspector Greg Foster, and I'm now in charge of this investigation. But I understand you've developed an excellent relationship with the missing woman's family."

"Tasha. The missing woman is Tasha Nkosi."

"Of course she is." Greg ploughed on, "So we'd like you to work alongside our family liaison officer, Inspector Sue Honeywell."

Keya was impressed that an inspector, rather than a constable was taking on the role.

"Please liaise with her."

Greg turned away from Keya.

"Sir."

He turned back. "Is there something else, Sergeant?" His tone made it clear he thought she was now wasting his valuable time.

"I need the national NHS number to access Tasha's medical records."

"I'm not sure that is necessary at this stage."

"Inspector Evans' instructions." Which wasn't exactly true, but he had asked her to investigate other angles in the case.

"Very well." He tapped his phone and then gave it to Keya. "Note this down, but don't give it to anyone else." Greg strode back to the group while Keya wrote the code down.

When she'd finished, she approached Chief Inspector Greg and waited while he gave instructions to two young constables.

"Yes," he sounded exasperated.

"Your phone," said Keya, holding it out and smiling sweetly.

She'd better find Inspector Honeywell, and then decide whether or not to stay for the community meeting.

The Inspector was a small, friendly lady wearing a floral summer dress. When Keya entered the reception area, she was consoling Linda. She turned to Keya and whispered, "Sergeant Varma?"

Keya nodded.

"Just give me a minute."

While Inspector Honeywell spoke earnestly with Linda, Keya glanced around the group.

Ezra was missing, and Nate was engrossed with his phone.

Solomon was shaking.

Keya sat down on the sofa next to him and said, "I know this is overwhelming, but these people are here to help. They're specialists."

"I know. And I am grateful. But I still don't believe my daughter would leave without telling any of us. What if something else has happened to her?"

"Do you mean if she is trapped somewhere, or has fallen and injured herself?" asked Keya.

He nodded. "Or someone has taken her?"

"This team will explore all possibilities," she consoled him. "And organise a comprehensive search to find her."

"Sergeant," called Inspector Honeywell, in a friendly tone.

Keya smiled at Solomon, before joining the inspector and moving away to stand beside the reception desk, which now had a black briefcase sitting on it.

"Thank you for speaking to Mr Nkosi. Our arrival has rattled his family." The inspector glanced across at them. "And I want to thank you for looking after them, and for arranging food, which is often overlooked. You've gained their trust, so I hope you'll continue to work with me."

"I'll help where I can. But I also have some work to do for my boss, Inspector Evans."

"Of course. I understand. Are you staying for the meeting?"

"Actually, I thought I'd head back to Coln Akeman. I left my sister there." For some reason, she didn't mention Ryan, or his involvement in the case.

"I understand, but can we talk later? I'll be here until late."

"Yes, of course." Keya didn't know when she'd return to Akemans but right now she wanted to find Ryan and Zivah, and to email The Elizabeth Blackwell Clinic.

CHAPTER TWENTY-ONE

Keya left Akemans auction house and tried to clear her head as she walked across the gravel car park.

Searching for Tasha Nkosi was no longer her responsibility, and neither was looking after Tasha's family.

Her thoughts were interrupted by a familiar voice.

"Why would they need to know about that?" Ezra Farmer stood beside his black SUV, his back to her, and she presumed he was talking to someone on his phone.

"No, I'm not saying anything, and neither should you. Tasha admitted it was a mistake, and I forgave her. That's all there is to it." Ezra's voice rose in anger.

He glanced around and Keya quickly ducked behind a white Transit van. She was starting to wonder about Ezra and if she'd been wrong about him. There might be more to Tasha's disappearance than he was letting on.

Should she interview him again? But what about? He wasn't going to admit what he was hiding, so she'd have to find out from someone else.

She emerged from behind the van, but Ezra was already striding towards the auction house.

Later. She'd speak to him later when she'd gathered more evidence. And he did seem genuinely concerned by Tasha's disappearance.

As she drove her car to Coln Akeman, she remembered other distraught husbands and boyfriends pleading for information about their missing loved ones at press conferences. But for a time, there had been a series of such instances where the men had actually been responsible for their partner's deaths. She hoped it wasn't true in this case.

Keya was pleased she wasn't driving her conspicuous police car as she spotted bored reporters gathered in groups on the village green, presumably looking to speak to people about Tasha. The inhabitants of Coln Akeman had presumably retreated indoors.

Keya parked behind The Axeman and called Zivah.

"Hi, sis. Where are you? And what's happening?" asked Zivah when she answered.

"Do you know where Ryan is?"

"Yes, with me. We're down the lane from the pub, searching for Tasha."

"Can you both meet me back at the pub?"

"Sure, and to be honest, I need a break. And I'm starving."

Keya heard another voice. Ryan's, she thought.

"And so is Ryan. See you in five."

Keya was surprised to find the pub relatively empty. Local men occupied the bar stools in the small snug, sipping their pints, but only four people were at a table in the main room at the front of the pub. Suspecting they were journalists, Keya chose the table in the bay window, well away from them, and waited for Ryan and Zivah to arrive.

As it was summer, a vase of dried flowers occupied the space in the large inglenook fireplace, where a welcome fire crackled in winter. Sunlight was catching the horse brasses decorating the black beams, highlighting molecules of dust clinging to strands of a spider's web.

"Oh, I'm shattered," exclaimed Zivah, flopping onto a wooden chair. "Ryan and I have looked in ditches, and searched hedgerows and footpaths, but there's no sign of Tasha. Have you had any luck?"

"Can we order food first, before comparing notes?" asked Ryan.

"Good idea." Zivah picked up a paper menu.

Keya glanced at it and remembered Friday was fish day. She never ate meat but occasionally she treated herself to fish, but she wasn't sure about Zivah.

"The battered fish and chips sounds great," her sister said. "But I hope I still need to fit into my wedding outfit next week."

"You've been walking all day," said Ryan. "Surely you've burned enough calories. And the fish and chips do sound good."

Zivah jumped to her feet. "Two fish and chips. Drinks?"

Keya and Ryan gave Zivah their orders and she approached the bar and spoke to a young man Keya hadn't seen before. She remembered the landlord was at the community meeting.

Keya leaned forward and said, "While my sister is busy, I need you to write an email including a special code which will authorise Tasha's doctor to release her medical information. But the code is super-secret. You mustn't tell anyone about it."

Ryan removed his phone and asked, "Who am I sending it to?"

Keya opened her notebook and turned it so he could read the address. She said, "Title it 'Urgent. Natasha Nkosi.' Then say something like 'Dear sir or madam. Further to my colleague, Sergeant Varma's call, I am seeking information from Natasha Nkosi's medical records. The authorisation code for my request is …'"

Keya tapped the code she'd written down. "'Provided by Chief Inspector Greg Foster.'"

Ryan looked up at Keya.

"I'll explain in a minute. Continue with, 'in particular we are looking for any information relevant to Natasha's disappearance including underlying mental health concerns or conditions. Also, can you confirm if Natasha is currently pregnant, or has recently been pregnant and sought a termination'."

Again, Ryan looked at Keya with a quizzical expression.

"Something a reporter asked me about, and I want to confirm it's true. Then say something along the lines of time being of the essence and you'd appreciate an immediate response."

Ryan tapped his phone and Keya looked up.

Zivah was standing beside the table. "Was Tasha …"

"We don't know. That's what we need to find out."

As Ryan completed and sent the email, Keya updated him and

Zivah on her interviews with Ezra and Tasha's family, and the arrival of the divisional team.

"So what's our role?" asked Ryan.

"I've been asked to assist the Family Liaison Officer, who seems very nice, but I didn't mention you to the Chief Inspector. Maybe you could help me? Inspector Evans wants me to consider all possibilities, including …"

Zivah gasped. "He doesn't think she's been murdered?"

The four men at the other table looked round at them.

"Shush," urged Keya, realising she was usually the one to attract attention by speaking loudly or saying something inappropriate. "Inspector Evans is not saying she has, but he wants to be prepared if we don't find her alive."

"Is this connected to the argument the neighbour told me about?" asked Ryan.

"That's certainly a consideration. Ezra denies he quarrelled with Tasha yesterday and I'm inclined to believe him. But if he didn't, who did? Especially the second argument, which was late, after she and Ezra returned from Cirencester. Ezra said he saw a car, probably a large saloon, parked beside the green. Now it might just have been a punter leaving the pub, but they turned their car lights off rather than on, so the driver might have been waiting for Ezra to leave."

"And then there's Tasha's pregnancy," whispered Zivah.

"Alleged pregnancy. But I overheard Ezra in the car park when I left Akemans. He sounded rattled and is clearly hiding something, which he told the person on the phone isn't relevant to this case."

"Which means it probably is," muttered Ryan.

The young man who had been behind the bar arrived with two white oval plates. On each was a large, battered fish and a huge pile of chips. He placed them on the table and said, "Sauces are there." He pointed to a wooden pot containing sauce sachets. "I'll just fetch your knives and forks."

Ryan picked up a chip, and Zivah and Keya followed his lead.

"Why didn't you order something?" Zivah asked her sister, looking at the chip Keya had removed from her plate.

"I had some sandwiches and didn't think I was hungry, but these chips are good."

"Aren't they?" grinned Zivah, picking up another and offering her plate to Keya.

The man returned with two sets of cutlery, rolled up in red paper napkins.

As Zivah and Ryan tucked into their fish, Keya dipped chips into tomato ketchup.

"So what's next?" asked Ryan.

"Did any of Tasha's other neighbours mention the arguing, or anything else unusual or suspicious?" asked Keya.

"No, but the old woman on the other side of Rose Cottage is very deaf."

Keya savoured a chip and thought about the case. "We have to tread very carefully," she said. "We don't want to interfere with the divisional team's investigation, and hamper their efforts to find Tasha, and we can't let the family know we're considering other possibilities at the moment. So how do we move forward?" she asked herself as she picked up another chip.

Then she asked Ryan, "Do you still have Tasha's phone?"

"Yes. And apart from looking at it for you earlier, I haven't had time to examine it properly."

"I don't think we'll get that opportunity, as I should deliver it to the Chief Inspector and his team. But let me have a look while you finish eating."

Ryan removed the phone and, remembering the passcode, tapped it in. "This is her call log." He slid the phone across to Keya.

There were a lot of missed calls. She scrolled through the recent ones which she presumed were from people trying to contact Tasha since she had disappeared, to those earlier in the day. Ezra had called several times and there were three missed calls from Tasha's father.

Keya scrolled back to Thursday. The last call was to her mum. Before that, she'd received one from someone called Naomi. Was that her sister, a friend, or someone else?

There was a missed call from her father and two calls from Ezra, which she'd answered. Tasha received plenty of calls from people but rarely made any, it seemed.

She hadn't rung the Samaritans. Keya hoped that was good news and Tasha hadn't felt suicidal or depressed enough to need their help.

Keya clicked onto one of the messaging apps on the phone. It showed the text conversation between her and Dan. She clicked on Dan's icon. There was no other information about him, so she jotted his number down in her notebook.

Returning to the text conversation, it was clear that Tasha was upset, missing her sister as she was the only person she could really talk to, and she was feeling under pressure. But pressure from whom?

Keya reread the whole text conversation. It appeared that the person who'd upset Tasha had done so after she and Zivah left Rose Cottage. If it was a phone call, then it would have been her father, Ezra, or Naomi, whoever she was. But what if the person had visited Tasha?

Out loud, Keya said, "We need to find out who the old man heard Tasha arguing with yesterday."

"OK," replied Ryan, stabbing the remaining piece of fish with his fork.

"And can you check if there's anything else of use on this phone before I hand it in? I've looked through her recent call log and that text message conversation with Dan."

Ryan took the phone back and swiped and clicked, before he said, "She has an email account on here."

"Write down the address. I don't suppose we can forward any emails to ourselves without the divisional team knowing?"

Ryan shook his head. "They'd know."

Ryan continued to swipe and click. "This is interesting. She has some photos of the local area, particularly the river. Oh look, here's one of a family of ducks swimming beside the reeds."

"Does she have any photos with people in them?"

Ryan scrolled and then turned the phone to Keya, who saw an image of two smiling young women.

"I presume that's Tasha with her sister," she said.

"Let's have a look." Zivah held her hand out for the phone.

Ryan passed it to her. "Sweet." She swiped and then drew in a deep breath. "Wow. Look at Tasha's wedding dress."

Keya leaned closer to her sister and peered at the phone. Tasha knew how to pose for a photo, and she looked stunning.

"Where are you?" Keya mumbled.

CHAPTER TWENTY-TWO

"OK," Keya checked her watch. Half past three on Friday afternoon. She said, "Ryan, you've had a long day. Do you want to continue door-to-door enquiries, or do you need to return to the station?"

Hesitating, Ryan pressed his lips together.

Zivah spoke for him, "He's going to Whitemead Forest Park this weekend with some friends. Who did you say's playing tomorrow night?"

Blushing, Ryan replied, "It's an Elvis tribute act."

"Are you getting dressed up?" asked Keya.

The colour in Ryan's cheeks deepened. "Yes."

"What fun!" cried Zivah.

"Then you should go back to the station and clock off," said Keya. "You've done a lot of legwork today." She looked from Ryan to Zivah. "You both have. Thank you. And we should let Chief Inspector Greg and his team handle the case now."

"What about Inspector Evans' instructions?" asked Ryan.

"I'll keep digging, but it's the weekend and we have important arrangements to make, don't we, Zivah?"

Zivah sat back in her chair. "Not tonight." She rubbed her forehead before asking, "Can I stay at yours? I feel like a girl's night curled up in your living room watching a film. But not a Bollywood one," she added hastily.

"What about Mum and Dad?" Keya asked.

"Exactly. All they'll want to do is ask questions and hassle me about the wedding."

"Fair point. And of course you can stay." Keya smiled. "It'll be fun." She pushed back her chair and stood up. "But first, let's hand in Tasha's phone and catch up with the case. Have a great weekend, Ryan."

"Thanks. You too."

"Bye," Zivah waved as Keya led the way through the snug and out through the low stone-arched doorway at the back of the pub. The car park was less than half full.

Keya drove to Akemans and once again parked in front of the antiques centre. "Do you want to come with me?"

Zivah shook her head. "No, I don't think that would be appropriate. I'll look round the antiques centre. How long will you be?"

"I'm not sure. But I'll try not to get tasked with anything else this afternoon. The only place I want to go now is home."

Solomon and Linda were still sitting on the grey sofa with mugs of tea or coffee in front of them on the wooden coffee table.

As Keya closed the reception door, Inspector Sue stood up and walked across to meet her. "Any news?"

Keya shook her head. "Nothing in the village. How are Tasha's parents?"

"I'm trying to persuade them to return to their hotel, but Solomon is refusing. He wants to wait here while the first search is conducted."

"First search?" What had she, Zivah, and Ryan been doing all day?

"Yes. Following the community meeting, there's going to be a search of the village, and the accessible roads and paths around it, this evening. If that doesn't yield anything, the police quad bikes and a specialist search and rescue team will join a more widescale search in the morning."

"It sounds as if you're going to be busy. When will you go home?" asked Keya.

"I won't. I have a room reserved in the same hotel as the Nkosis, so I can be on hand."

Keya glanced down at Inspector Sue's hand, checking for a wedding ring. She wore a simple gold band and an engagement ring made up of three diamonds.

Inspector Sue smiled. "My husband is used to me being away, and this evening is quiz night down at our local. Since he retired, he's kept himself busy with an allotment and he joined the village bowls club. He even put himself on a cooking course, which is fantastic, as I don't have to think about what to feed us every night when I get home from work."

The door to the auction room opened and a preoccupied Chief Inspector Greg passed them, speaking on his phone. "I am sorry to miss Lottie's concert tonight, but this case …"

"Oh dear," said Inspector Sue. "The Chief Inspector's wife is not so understanding about his absences. But then he does have younger children."

"Is Nick, I mean Sergeant Unwin, still here?"

"Yes, he's in the auction room with the rest of the media team."

"Media team?" repeated Keya, wondering how many of them there were.

"Yes, a recent report highlighted that it's crucial to seek help from the public on social media for missing person cases. Although, it's less important this time as the disappearance is already on the national news. But the media team put together a profile and enough information on the missing person to persuade the public to help, without divulging anything sensitive. And maintaining that balance is often a challenge."

"I can imagine," Keya agreed.

"As is how much exposure we give the family. At the moment, Tasha's parents want to maintain their privacy, but Ezra and her brother are happy to speak to the press if we think it will help."

"And will it?" queried Keya.

"That's a decision the Chief Inspector will make tomorrow. If the searches don't turn up anything."

Keya was impressed. The team appeared organised, efficient, and calm.

The front door of the auction room opened, and Chief Inspector Greg stormed back in, clenching his jaw.

"Sir," said Keya as he strode past.

"What?" he answered sharply. He stopped and made a visible effort to calm himself. "Sorry, Sergeant. How can I help?"

Keya handed him Tasha's phone. "This was in Rose Cottage. Nate, Tasha's brother, admitted he knew the passcode - 77977 by the way - and we checked her calls and messages. But I thought your team might find more on it than we did."

"Thank you, Sergeant. We were wondering where this was. I'll have someone examine it straight away. And what about you?"

"If it's OK, I'm going home. I have my sister with me and we've both had a long day." Keya smiled at Inspector Sue. "And I think you have everything covered."

"Thank you for your help, Sergeant. And call in over the weekend if you have any news, or want an update." Chief Inspector Greg strode across to the auction room door.

Keya turned to Inspector Sue and said, "Good luck."

CHAPTER TWENTY-THREE

Knock, knock.

Keya woke and heard the sound again.

Knock, knock.

Someone was tapping on her bedroom door.

"Sis, are you awake? I've made you a cup of coffee."

It was Zivah. She'd stayed last night after they'd watched a film about a grumpy old man who'd been befriended by a family and died happy.

Perhaps not the best choice, but there hadn't been many alternatives after Zivah rejected all the romance and murder mystery films, and neither of them had felt like watching a fast-paced action adventure movie.

"Keya, are you awake?" Zivah asked sharply.

"Yes," groaned Keya.

The door opened and Zivah entered, carrying two mugs. She placed one on the bedside table and sat down on Keya's bed, cradling the other. "How did you sleep?"

"Well, until someone woke me up." Keya sank her head back down on the pillows.

Zivah waited.

"And how did you sleep?" asked Keya, knowing it was the expected response.

"Not well. It was all very well spending yesterday searching for Tasha, and I know it had to be done, but what hope is there for my wedding now? It's the weekend. By the time we contact the marquee companies it'll be Monday, and the wedding is supposed to be on Friday. How can it possibly go ahead?"

Zivah had clearly woken up stressed.

"It's OK. Marquee companies work weekends in the summer. We'll go through the list I found last night from the Christmas ball and phone round this morning. I'm sure one of them can help us out."

"And what about the food?"

"What's the one thing Indian women are good at?" asked Keya.

"Cooking," smiled Zivah.

"If the worst happens, and we can't find a suitable caterer, we'll just ask the family. I'm sure everyone will be happy to help out. And I can ask my friend Kuki to provide some dishes. And as I'm no longer on Tasha's case, I can cook this week too."

"But what about your cafe?"

"That can wait. You're more important."

"Thanks, sis." Zivah smiled.

Keya's phone rang and Zivah's smile faded.

Pulling herself into a sitting position, Keya answered the call. "Ryan, what are you doing up so early?"

"It's half past eight."

"Is it? I must have slept in. Which is what I thought you would be doing."

"No, we're playing golf this morning."

Keya shook her head. Did Ryan ever rest?

"Look, I've had a call from Ozzie this morning and she's in a bit of a quandary. Can you meet her at The Old Boathouse at The Cotswold Waterpark in half an hour?"

"Half an hour! I'm still in bed."

Zivah stood up and left the room.

"This is important," insisted Ryan.

"OK. Tell her I'll be there in forty-five minutes."

Keya finished the call and pulled herself out of bed. She tripped over her slippers. "Oh toda!"

Twenty minutes later, she was in her car driving to meet Ozzie. Keya presumed Ozzie wanted to see her because she was reporting on Tasha's missing person case. If so, Keya wasn't sure what she could tell her, except that she needed to contact the official media team.

Zivah had opted to stay behind and call the marquee companies on Keya's list, but she'd begged Keya not to be away too long. And Zivah was right. Would they find a marquee, and tables, chairs, and everything else that was needed for a wedding, in less than a week?

Keya gripped the steering wheel. They'd just have to try.

The Old Boathouse was purpose-built, with low-level stone walls and, above them, horizontal slats of grey wood. Inside, it was light and airy.

Keya found Ozzie waiting for her at a table beside the full height glass doors, which looked out over a raised balcony and the lake beyond.

Ozzie had her laptop open in front of her. She looked up and smiled. "Order yourself a drink and put it on my tab."

Returning with a cappuccino, Keya sat down as Ozzie closed her laptop.

Ozzie said, "Thanks for meeting me, and sorry to wake you up."

"You didn't, my sister did. For a week off, it's been surprisingly busy."

"I understand you met up with the missing woman again, after we saw her briefly at The Axeman."

Keya hesitated, not sure what to say.

Ozzie smiled. "Don't worry, this isn't an interview, although I have been asked by a London paper to report on the case." Her smiled broadened, and then faded. "But I'm in a dilemma, which is why I phoned Ryan."

Ozzie paused, and Keya sipped her coffee.

Ozzie continued, "I'll come straight to the point. Someone close to Tasha Nkosi, I don't know who, wants to sell their story."

"Their story?" queried Keya.

"Sorry, they have information about Tasha, personal information, which they want to sell."

Keya thought immediately about the question of Tasha's pregnancy, wondering if Ryan had heard back from the medical practice. She'd phone him later, when he'd finished his golf.

"I was right. There is information the police are holding back."

Keya looked directly at Ozzie and said, "There always is."

"I've been told the source said that Tasha was not the excited bride-to-be, and they hinted that she might have some mental health and alcohol issues."

"They what?" exclaimed Keya.

"So it's not true."

"Ozzie, you know I can't confirm or deny suggestions like that. You'll have to go through the proper channels, but I doubt they will say any more than I can."

Ozzie held her hands up in a conciliatory gesture.

"Look, I understand. I reported on that case last year when a fifteen-year-old girl vanished. If that TV channel hadn't alleged her stepfather was abusing her, the police might have found her much earlier, and without all the speculation that she'd been murdered."

Keya nodded. Remembering the case. The TV channel had been wrong.

Ozzie continued, "Like you, my main concern is the missing woman and her family. In last year's case, the girl's mother and stepfather split up, and he was forced to move abroad."

Ozzie took a deep breath. "I think the family should be made aware of the allegations and decide for themselves whether to tell the press or not. But this is a huge opportunity for me. I might even secure a job in London with one of the national papers if I get it right."

"What do you want me to do?"

"I'll have to run with the story, but if, while I'm preparing it, the police release a statement, then it won't appear so damning and hopefully the paper won't pay the rat who leaked it."

"I'll speak to Nick, Sergeant Unwin. He's still involved with the case, and he's working as part of the media team. How long have we got?"

"My deadline is one o'clock."

Keya gulped. That was less than four hours.

Ozzie tapped the table. "And in return, is there anything you can tell me?"

Keya wrinkled her nose. Was there always a price to pay? But Ozzie was risking her job and her reputation by telling her about the tip. Was there something that Ozzie could report that would help the case?

"One of Tasha's neighbours told Ryan he heard her having a row with a man on Thursday. You might want to ask him about it, and see if anyone else saw or heard anything which would identify this man."

"And if I do, should I tell you?"

"You could just send me a link to your article."

Ozzie laughed. "I'll do that."

CHAPTER TWENTY-FOUR

When Keya left Ozzie at The Old Boathouse, she thought of phoning Nick to tell him about Ozzie's story but decided it would be better to talk to him face-to-face.

Sighing, and feeling guilty about not helping Zivah, she climbed into her car and drove to Akemans.

The front door of the auction house was open, but the reception area was empty. Hearing voices, Keya opened the door into the auction room and gasped. It had been transformed.

A large screen stood on the raised stage, and it was currently divided into four sections with what looked like different news stories playing in each.

All the tables and chairs Gilly had gathered together for the cafe were arranged in groups around the auction room. Most were currently empty, although on several, a single person was sitting working on a laptop.

But the corner where Gilly set up her cafe during an auction was humming. The chairs around two pushed-together tables were full and Nick was leaning over a desk and looking at a screen while a younger officer tapped keys.

He looked up at Keya and gave her a quizzical expression.

She smiled back apologetically and inclined her head towards an empty area of the room.

Nick joined her and asked, "What's happened?"

"I've just had a tip off from Ozzie Winters."

"The journalist?" Nick narrowed his eyes at her.

"Hey, she called me, and I didn't tell her anything about the case." The row the neighbour had overheard wasn't technically to do with the missing person case, she tried to convince herself.

"And?" demanded Nick.

Irritated, Keya looked up and held Nick's gaze. "You have a leak. Someone close to the case has sold their story to a national newspaper, telling them that Tasha had mental health issues and an alcohol problem."

"They've what?" thundered Nick. "Who is it?"

"I don't think Ozzie knew. But if she did, she didn't tell me."

"What can we do?"

"Ozzie told me she'd delay the story until one o'clock. Which gives you," she checked her watch, "just over three hours."

"Three hours." Nick ran his hand through his thick black hair. Keya noticed it wasn't as immaculately coiffed as usual.

"I guess you have two choices. Either the paper Ozzie's writing for leaks the story, or you put out a press release and regain the narrative. If that's the correct term to use," Keya said.

Nick looked at her with a note of respect in his eyes. "You should go on that media course. That's exactly the term to use. And you're right. We, and not the press, need to control the information which is released. I'll prepare a couple of variations of a statement and contact Chief Inspector Greg."

"Where is he?" asked Keya, glancing around the large room.

"Directing today's extended search party. I keep hoping someone will call in with good news, but we haven't heard anything yet."

Keya's phone buzzed. It was Gilly Wimsey.

"Thanks, Keya," Nick said as he patted her on the shoulder and walked away.

Keya answered Gilly's call. "Keya, a man keeps trying to climb into the garden, and the kids are out playing."

"Hi, Gilly. The police in charge of the case are running an extensive search today. Maybe someone is being a little too enthusiastic."

"Enthusiastic. Then why is he filming with his phone on the end of a stick? It's not right."

Keya agreed. It did sound weird.

"I'll come over." She convinced herself Coln Akeman was on her way home. Just as long as she didn't stay too long.

As Keya entered the village, she spotted a white Land Rover Defender parked beside the village green. Two people with red tops with 'search and rescue' printed on the back, were studying something, presumably a map, on the car's bonnet. There was a figure with a shaved head with them, who resembled Chief Inspector Greg.

She turned off the main road and parked outside Gilly and Dr Peter Wimsey's Victorian two-storey house with a pair of bay windows. There wasn't any sign of the search being conducted on this street. Before ringing the doorbell, she took the footpath which ran along the side of the property to a wood behind it.

Spotting her, a man stepped out of the wood holding a mobile phone on the end of a metal rod.

"Did you ever meet Natasha Nkosi?" he demanded.

"Who are you?" countered Keya.

"I'm Detective Otto," replied the overweight, bearded man.

"You're a police officer?"

The man puffed out his chest. "I'm …" he hesitated, "a digital detective."

Keya wrinkled her nose. "Well I'm the real deal. Sergeant Varma, and you're upsetting local people. Please collect your things and move on."

Otto backed away and then stopped and planted his feet. "I'm not doing any harm, and this is a public right of way."

"But the garden isn't." Keya pointed at the post and rail fence which surrounded the Wimsey's garden. "And you were spotted trying to climb over it."

"But Natasha Nkosi might be lying injured or being kept captive."

"Captive? Don't be ridiculous. And if she is injured, this is the best place for her. It's the home of the local doctor."

"I didn't know that. But the public want to know she's OK."

"As do her parents and fiancé, and the public can certainly help by looking out for her and giving the police any information they have. But the police need to co-ordinate the search for her, with the assistance of the local community. Doing your own thing is not helping, it's only upsetting people."

Otto lowered the metal rod and removed his phone. "I don't want to upset people. I only want to help." He looked down at the dry earth of the footpath.

Keya had a sudden thought. "You can help. Are you good with computers?"

"Of course." Otto sounded affronted that she might think otherwise.

"There's so much going on now, as everyone is concerned about Miss Nkosi's disappearance. But what about last week, or last month?"

"You think something happened which led to her vanishing?"

"People don't walk out without a reason. And she has been in the public eye for her modelling and upcoming wedding. I don't know if she was a party girl back in London."

Otto beamed. "I could find out. She's sure to have posted photos. Most glamourous young women do."

"Then maybe you should start there. And see if you can find out anything which actually helps the police."

Otto placed his phone back on the rod and held it up. "Can I say I'm assisting the police with their enquiries?"

"You can say that all members of the public who discover anything relating to the whereabouts of Natasha Nkosi should immediately contact the helpline."

Otto lowered the rod. "That's not a great soundbite."

Keya handed him her card. "I'm not concerned with soundbites, but with real life and death situations."

Otto smiled. "That's more like it!"

Keya shook her head. "Now, please leave." She waited for Otto to return items to a black rucksack, which he then picked up, and she accompanied him back to the street.

"Where's your car?"

"Car? I'm walking home." Otto turned and trudged away from Keya.

Keya shook her head as she watched him. He was a local. Then surely he knew who the Wimseys were. So why loiter around their garden?

Keya walked to the side of the house and rang the doorbell. She heard footsteps and felt someone on the other side of the door. Were they peering through the spy hole?

"Oh, it's you, Keya," cried Gilly as she swung the door open. "Is that man still at the end of the garden?"

"No, and I've spoken to him. Do you know he lives in the village?"

"Really, I've never seen him before. Come in."

Keya followed Gilly down the hallway.

"Thomas, Olivia, you can go outside now. That man's gone." As they entered the kitchen, Gilly said, "My father bought them a swing ball, which they love playing with. And I'm happy as it means they're occupied and outside in the fresh air. Tea? Coffee?"

"I'd love a cup of tea, but I can't stay long. I'm supposed to be helping Zivah find a marquee for her wedding."

Keya updated Gilly on Zivah's wedding disaster and their visit to Windrush Hall.

"Sounds like there's a lot to organise in, what, five days?"

"I know, but if everyone pulls together, I'm sure we can do it. And now Chief Inspector Greg's team has taken over Tasha's case, I can help Zivah."

"The auction room lends itself very well to being a centre of police operations. I should take photos and send them to location agencies. Mind you, George would have a fit if the auction house was overrun by film crews. But it would be a useful source of extra income," mused Gilly as the electric kettle boiled.

While Gilly made tea, Keya checked her phone. Ryan had messaged telling her to check her emails, so she did. He'd forwarded her the reply from Tasha's doctor's surgery.

Keya opened the email and gasped.

CHAPTER TWENTY-FIVE

The word 'foetus' jumped out of Tasha's doctor's notes at Keya. Tasha was pregnant. But there were lots of abbreviations and groups of capital letters which she didn't understand. Perhaps they were deliberately baffling, so only a doctor could read the notes. A doctor.

"Is Dr Peter here?" asked Keya.

"Yes, he's just fitting a shelf in Olivia's room. I'll call him. I'm sure he'd like a cup of tea." Gilly stepped into the hallway and shouted, "Peter!"

Keya heard shouting and laughing from the back garden.

As Gilly swept papers and magazines to one side on the kitchen table and set down mugs of tea, Dr Peter entered the kitchen.

He ran a hand through his sandy coloured hair and observed Keya. "Good morning, Sergeant. We're not in trouble, are we?"

"Gilly called me about a man trying to enter the garden ..."

"Who Keya sent on his way. Can you believe he actually lives in the village?" Gilly sounded affronted.

"Well done, but if that's all, I'll take my tea upstairs." Dr Peter picked up his mug.

"There was something," said Keya, opening the email on her phone. "Can you decipher these patient's notes for me?"

"I take it this is a police matter, and you have the practice's consent."

"Yes, we used the national code which Chief Inspector Greg gave us."

"Then these must be Natasha Nkosi's notes," said Dr Peter, holding out his hand for Keya's phone.

He read through them muttering "poor girl" and "oh dear".

Gilly sat down as both she and Keya watched Dr Peter in silence.

Eventually he said, "I can understand why she ran away. She recently lost a baby, which may have had a huge impact, mentally."

"She lost the baby. Oh, poor Tasha," groaned Keya. Then she asked, "Lost, not terminated?"

"I don't think I should be listening to this," said Gilly, starting to stand up.

Keya laid a hand on her arm. "Probably not, but you might be able to help."

Gilly lowered herself back into her chair as Dr Peter nodded and said, "Yes, at the eleven-week point."

"Does it say anything about the father?" asked Keya.

"Surely that would be Ezra, unless you know differently?" said Gilly.

"I don't know much about Tasha's background, but I'm trying to find out."

"Why? Surely Chief Inspector Greg is running the case now," said Gilly.

"The missing person's one, yes."

Gilly rubbed her chin, looking confused.

Keya hesitated.

"Ah," voiced Dr Peter. "It's his case while it remains a missing person one. But if Natasha Nkosi turns up, and she's not alive, then he won't be in charge."

"Something like that," agreed Keya. She still didn't want to jinx the search by talking about Tasha as if she was dead.

Dr Peter cleared his throat. "All these notes say is that when Tasha joined this surgery, she was pregnant. She had an initial scan and follow-up appointments but at the eleven week point she reported feeling cramps and noticed a discharge. The doctor confirmed it was a miscarriage."

"And do they mention anything about her mental wellbeing?"

"This doctor only saw her once more, a week later, and she was understandably upset. It says here she was advised to rest and take things easy."

"I wonder if that's why she rented a cottage in the village," said Keya. "So she could recover in peace."

"It makes sense," agreed Gilly. "But to be all alone. It won't have been good for her."

"No," Keya agreed. "I hope she confided in her sister. The way she talked about her, they seemed very close." She checked her black watch. "And talking of sisters, I better go and help mine with her wedding plans."

Keya took her phone back from Dr Peter. "Thank you. For the explanation, and the tea. And hopefully, nobody else will try to search your garden looking for Tasha."

"If she was hiding in the shed, I'm sure she wouldn't stay long with the racket the kids are making," Dr Peter remarked.

Gilly showed Keya to the door and said, "I hope you sort everything out for Zivah's wedding. Will you be on site on Monday for the erection of the waterwheel?"

Keya had forgotten all about it.

"I hope so, but I do have to go into the station first thing. Team meetings and all that."

Keya drove home, feeling dejected. If only she and Zivah had known about Tasha's lost baby, they might have been able to comfort her.

Derek and Peggy were sitting on a bench in their garden watching Winston run about when Keya arrived home. She waved at them, and Peggy stood up and wandered across to the hedge. "You know I mentioned that hospital appointment?" she said.

"Oh, yes."

"Well, it's on Wednesday morning, and Derek reckons he's promised to help make hay if the weather remains dry. Would you be able to drive me to Cheltenham?"

"Yes, of course, but you know how forgetful I can be, especially with so much going on. Remind me again on Tuesday."

"Any news of that missing lass?" asked Peggy.

"I'm afraid not. There's an extensive search being conducted at the moment, so let's hope she turns up."

"I saw your colleague on the telly. Not the young one, the darker, attractive one."

"Nick. Sergeant Unwin?"

"That's him. Well, he said that the family is concerned about the missing woman because she has mental health issues, poor dear. I do hope they find her soon."

So Nick had persuaded Chief Inspector Greg to take the initiative and reveal Tasha's condition before Ozzie's story broke.

Her phone pinged, and she checked her messages. "Thanks for the tip. See attached for an update."

Keya was about to open the link and then she thought of Zivah. She'd better catch up with her sister before heading down another rabbit hole in Tasha's case.

As she opened the front door, Zivah cried, "Keya. I've found a marquee."

Keya smiled with relief.

She found Zivah in the kitchen and sat down at the table, saying, "Well done. Tell me about it."

"It's a company in Oxford. The local show they're supplying tents for next weekend doesn't need as many as they ordered, so they can provide a marquee, with tables and chairs, for two hundred people."

"Is that enough?"

"Just. We're up to a hundred and ninety-six. I'll just have to make sure neither mum invites any last-minute guests." Zivah smiled indulgently. "And they've also given me the number for a company who supplies cutlery and crockery, and tablecloths. I was about to ring them when you walked in."

"Then don't let me stop you."

Zivah joined Keya at the small kitchen table. She dialled a number and when her call was answered, she said, "Mark at Oxford Marquees suggested I call you."

As Zivah explained what she needed, Keya opened the link Ozzie had sent her.

There was a profile on Tasha and quotes from a couple of her friends. They both said she was a lively, outgoing young woman, but kind and considerate as well. However, they'd seen less of her during the past few months, which they put down to her preparing for her wedding. Only one of them knew she was staying in the Cotswolds.

Then there was the information from the person close to Tasha who claimed she'd been struggling mentally, wasn't eating properly, and she'd been drinking more than usual.

Ozzie had worded it in such a way that it didn't appear too damning, and she painted a picture of someone who was anxious and nervous about her impending wedding, rather than someone depressed or suicidal.

"For two hundred," said Zivah.

Keya sat up as she read the next paragraph. Ozzie had written that the day before Tasha's disappearance two young men visited her, who were not her fiancé. The first was identified as her brother, Nate, who was visiting with his parents from London.

But neighbours heard raised voices and Nate was spotted storming out of her cottage. The identity of the second man, who arrived after midnight, is unknown.

Keya leaned back. Why hadn't Nate told her he'd visited Tasha on his own? Was he worried his parents would discover he'd argued with his sister? And what were they quarrelling about?

And the young man who'd been spotted after midnight might have been Dan, her fit-out contractor, making good on his promise to come over after his exchange of text messages with Tasha. Keya hoped he'd come forward and tell Chief Inspector Greg's team about his visit.

But had there been another visitor after Tasha and Ezra returned from Cirencester? Ozzie hadn't mentioned anyone, but the neighbours might not have spotted him, especially if he didn't want to be seen.

"Thank you so much," said Zivah, finishing her call.

"Isn't that great?"

"What?" asked Keya.

"Weren't you listening? That company can provide all the crockery and cutlery we need. Now we need to sort out the food. I've written down the names of several companies who've been recommended. Can you help me look at them?"

"Of course," replied Keya, pushing thoughts of Tasha's visitors away. "Where shall we start?"

CHAPTER TWENTY-SIX

Keya had planned to sleep in again on Sunday morning, as she expected the following week to be full and tiring.

But instead, she woke feeling fully awake and refreshed at seven o'clock. After showering and getting dressed, she wandered downstairs and switched on the kettle.

Zivah had gone home to their parent's house the night before, but not before Keya had promised to visit for Sunday lunch. She suspected Zivah wanted her moral support.

Keya stretched and smiled. She had the whole morning to work on her cafe menu. Picking up a yellow cardboard folder from a pile on the end of her kitchen counter, she emptied the contents onto the table and started reading through the notes she'd made.

Had she really started these back in January after attending an afternoon tea cookery course?

She didn't plan to serve burgers or chips, but stick to simple healthy dishes such as sandwiches, baked potatoes, homemade soups, and variations of salads. She thought she might try several different salads to see which her customers preferred.

She could batch cook soup and keep some in the fridge and the rest in the freezer. She searched for her list of soup ideas.

Keya spent the morning happily engrossed in food recipes. Realising her coffee was cold, she checked her watch.

"Oh toda!" she exclaimed out loud. It was a quarter past twelve and she'd promised to be at her parents' for half past.

Leaving her paperwork scattered across the table, she grabbed her phone, bag, and car keys, and left the house. She ran down the garden path through the drizzle, jumped into her car, and drove to her parents' house in Gloucester.

When Keya walked into her parent's kitchen, her hair damp from the rain, her mum proclaimed, "At last. I thought you were helping Zivah make chapatis?"

"Was I? Sorry, I finally had a few hours to work on my cafe menus and didn't realise what the time was."

"Are you sure you don't want to serve traditional Indian food? I could help with the recipes."

It was a question her mother always asked.

"Thanks, Mum, but it's not what visitors to the antiques centre want. Although I'd like to introduce some Indian cakes at some point."

Keya's mum smiled. "Your grandmother made the best honey cake."

Keya smiled back. She remembered enjoying the cake on a trip to her grandparents when she was only five or six.

"I'm ready," said Keya's mum, wiping her hands on her apron. "We're just waiting for Aadi. Can you check Maitri has set the table properly?"

Aadi arrived ten minutes later, looking tense and unusually agitated. While Keya and her parents and younger sister waited in the living room, Aadi and Zivah moved into the hall.

Keya heard Zivah cry, "No, not after all my hard work."

"Oh, dear," muttered Keya's dad. "That didn't sound good."

A few minutes later, Aadi escorted a sniffling Zivah back into the living room. Without preamble, he announced, "I'm afraid we're postponing the wedding. The priest now says this is an unlucky week and we should wait until the next nakshatra, which isn't until next month."

"I can't believe it. Not after all the hard work we've done, Keya," wailed Zivah.

Keya moved across to Zivah as Aadi removed his arm from around her shoulders. Holding her clasped hands, Keya said, "Maybe it's for the best, sis. It will give us time to make sure your wedding is exactly as you and Aadi want it. We've so much to do. The days will fly by."

"But what about all the invitations? How can we tell everyone we've changed the date and the venue?"

Aadi assured her, "I wouldn't worry about that. All the relatives and most of our friends understand that if the priest says the stars aren't aligned, then the wedding shouldn't go ahead. It's bad karma."

"I suppose so," sniffed Zivah.

CHAPTER TWENTY-SEVEN

On Monday morning, Keya joined Ryan in their team room at Cirencester Police Station.

"How was the weekend?" she asked.

"Great fun. You should come with us next time. There's an ABBA tribute band playing."

Keya didn't know what to think. She was touched to be invited, but music wasn't really her thing. Mind you, she did need to get out and do more than work, whether it be for the police or her cafe.

"I'll think about it, but if it's next month, I won't be able to. Zivah's had to move her wedding."

"But I thought she was using Windrush Hall."

"She was, and maybe still is. But her fiancé's parents and the priest have decided that the proposed wedding day is bad luck, probably because of what's happened to Tasha. So the wedding has been postponed until next month."

"Your poor sister. She must be upset."

"She was, but then she agreed that changing the venue and sorting out a marquee and the food was stressful, and that another month would ease the pressure."

Keya heard voices from behind Inspector Evans' closed office door. "Who's he with?" she asked.

"Nick, and they're having a conference call with Chief Inspector Greg. After that, Nick's updating us on Tasha's case. And apart from her disappearance, it's been a blessedly quiet weekend. We don't have any new cases."

"Good. Rowan and his team are putting the new waterwheel in today, so I want to visit Akemans, and we have another fit-out meeting."

"Fit-out. Does that mean Dan will be there?"

"Exactly my thoughts. I can ask him about his visit to Rose Cottage. That's if Tasha is still missing?"

"She is. The only sign of her was the gold heart and chain which she wore around her neck."

"The one Ezra gave her? Where was it?"

"Beside a bench on the river footpath."

"Was it intact, or had the chain been broken?"

"I'm not sure."

The door to Inspector Evan's office flew open and Nick emerged. "Hi, sorry, I have to rush off. A woman's been spotted in Bristol who fits Natasha Nkosi's description."

Nick ran out and Keya and Ryan turned to look at Inspector Evans, who stood in his doorway, a brooding expression on his face. "I hope this isn't a hoax."

Inspector Evans, rather than Nick, updated Keya and Ryan on Tasha's case, which was only that she was still missing. They also discussed the progress of other ongoing investigations.

As there wasn't much, Keya didn't feel guilty about leaving the police station and driving to Akemans.

She entered the antiques centre, ignoring the auction house, and walked through to the cafe space. Hearing shouts from outside, she walked out of the old mill and found Rowan and his team constructing the wooden waterwheel.

To make it work, the central section had to connect to various metal rods which were, in turn, attached to large cogs and machinery inside the old mill. It was this central section Rowan and his team were manoeuvring into place.

Keya joined Vic and Gilly on the riverbank as they watched the activity.

"Apparently, this is the tricky part," Vic said. "Once the barrel is in place, the rest of the wheel is easy to construct. They might even finish today."

"And then can we open the sluice gates and let water back into the channel?" asked Keya.

"Yes. We've repaired the wall and fitted a new sluice gate, so we're ready to go."

"I feel we should have an opening ceremony," enthused Gilly.

"Maybe we can. When the cafe opens. But we'll need to test it all works first," said Keya, practically. She wasn't ready for an opening ceremony.

Vic said, "Dan should be here. Shall we go inside and finalise the cafe fit-out?"

Keya and Gilly followed Vic back into the old mill building.

"I hope the police will have finished with the tables and chairs by the time we open, or customers won't have anywhere to sit," said Gilly.

"I'm not sure how these things work, but I expect the investigation will be scaled down if she hasn't been found after a week, and the team will continue their enquiries out of their Gloucester headquarters."

"Or pass the case back to you," suggested Gilly.

"Possibly."

Keya sat through the meeting listening to discussions on wall colours, the final position of electrical power sockets and lighting for the cafe area.

"I think the metal dome pendant lights," said Gilly. "What do you think, Keya?"

"They certainly fit in with the history and feel of the building."

After forty-five minutes the meeting drew to a close and Keya approached Dan, who was packing plans away into his canvas briefcase.

"I wondered if I could talk to you about Tasha," said Keya. "You must be very upset that just after you two reconnected, she disappeared."

Dan stopped what he was doing and looked at Keya. She saw genuine concern in his eyes. "You saw what she was like last week at the pub. So panicky, she nearly got herself run over. What if she did that again? And this time she was knocked over, or she may have fallen down a well or …"

"Dan," said Keya in a calm, but authoritative voice. "The police conducted a full-scale search over the weekend, and they'll have checked all the hospitals and all the wells, ditches and hedges for miles around."

Dan bowed his head. Either in relief or acknowledgement, Keya didn't know.

"How was she when you last saw her? The night before she disappeared?" asked Keya gently.

"Upset." Dan raised his head, and his eyes were large and frightened. "But how did you know about that?"

"She left her phone, and we read your messages. I'm surprised the police team running the search hasn't contacted you."

"They have, but I lied. I said I meant to go over on Friday, but by the time I got there she'd gone."

"Why lie?" asked Keya.

Dan's shoulders drooped. "How do you think it looks? An old friend, a single man, back in her life and with the pregnancy. What would everyone think?"

"You knew about that?" Keya's voice rose in surprise.

"Not to start with. But after that incident at the pub, I went back and sat with Tasha, in silence to start with. But eventually she started talking and when she did, she couldn't stop. She told me about the pressure from her family to marry Ezra, and from his family to have the perfect fairytale wedding. She said everyone treated her like a doll, like an innocent child, and she tried her best to be what they wanted, but it didn't work."

Dan halted, just as Keya thought she was about to learn more about Tasha. Another side. "She rebelled?"

"Not exactly, but she did go out with a group of models and the photography crew after a photo shoot, and one thing led to another.

She admitted she didn't really enjoy the parties or the drinking. I'm not sure if she took drugs as well, but she said the parties were wild and she was out of control, but in a strange way it felt good. Freeing, and she was swept up in the hype, the glamour and the fame. They were the party set and their photos were in the right magazines and all over social media."

"And?" pressed Keya when Dan paused again.

"But," said Dan. "Let's go outside."

Keya followed him out of the mill building and as they stood on the paved area for the outdoor seating, looking out over the river, Dan said, "But Tasha told me that, after a particularly wild party, she woke up in bed with the assistant editor of a magazine. A much older man. And she had no idea how she got there and no recollection of the night."

Keya asked gently, "Was he the father of the baby?"

"Tasha thought so, although her and Ezra have been intimate, so ultimately she wasn't sure."

"Did she tell anyone?"

"She was so worried about what her family would say that she moved doctors' clinics."

Of course, thought Keya. Moving to the Elizabeth Blackwell Clinic now made sense.

Dan continued, "But she finally told her sister, who persuaded her to speak to Ezra."

"And did she?" asked Keya.

"Yes, and Tasha said he was so understanding, it just made her feel worse. Together they decided to keep the baby, so when she lost it, she was devastated. She told me it was like losing part of her soul."

"And that's when she rented the cottage in the Cotswolds."

"Yes, to be closer to Ezra, but not so close to his family that they could pop in whenever they felt like it. I also think Ezra wanted her away from the modelling party crowd, as they were pestering Tasha to go out with them again."

That all made sense and tied in with what Keya already knew.

"But you did see her the night before she vanished?"

"Yes. She was really upset. It was late, but we had been good friends, and I knew how vulnerable she was."

When Dan didn't say any more, Keya asked, "And did she tell you who had upset her?"

"No. But I had the impression it had something to do with the wedding. She kept going on about the pressure she was under, and couldn't everyone leave her alone. It was her wedding, so couldn't she decide what she wanted? I'm not convinced she actually wanted the wedding."

Keya raised her eyebrows as she queried, "Tasha doesn't want to marry Ezra?"

"No, I think she does. But not at the huge fairy-tale wedding his parents have organised. They've invited all the influential people they want to impress, but as it's on Friday, most of her friends are working and can't come. Ezra said they'd have another party in London, but for Tasha, I don't think it was the same."

Keya gazed out over the flowing river water before asking, "So what do you think has happened? Where is Tasha?"

Dan slowly drew in a breath as he also studied the river. "I honestly don't know."

CHAPTER TWENTY-EIGHT

Keya woke on Tuesday morning and prepared to go to work. She'd agreed with Inspector Evans that, as her sister's wedding had been postponed, she'd work Tuesday, Wednesday and Thursday, and catch up with her Rural Enforcement jobs.

This meant going to the station to answer emails, and to organise visits to schools, clubs, and local events.

The rest of the time she'd spend patrolling the area and visiting farmers. It was important to maintain a presence to deter vandals and thieves, although with over a thousand square kilometres to cover, this was an impossible task.

In the kitchen, she glanced at her stack of cafe folders. She'd made great progress the last couple of days and had lots of ideas for her menus.

Next, she needed to decide which items to trial as permanent menu items and which ones to rotate as specials. Hopefully she could sit down and sort that out after work one night this week.

As she closed the front door and walked down her garden path, she heard Peggy call, "Keya, don't forget tomorrow."

Keya had forgotten.

"What time do you want to leave?" Keya asked.

"My appointment's at quarter past nine. And I don't want to be late. Is eight o'clock OK with you?"

"That's fine," said Keya, although she must remember to tell the inspector she'd be busy in the morning.

As she opened the garden gate, her phone rang. It was Gilly.

"Hiya," she said, as she answered the call.

"Keya, you must come. Something awful has happened."

"Not another dead body?"

The previous month, they'd found several bodies at Akemans and Gilly was the one who'd called with the bad news. But it couldn't have happened again, could it?

"I'm not sure what it is, but Rowan called me, and he's really spooked."

"I thought Rowan's team finished the installation of the waterwheel yesterday."

"They did. But he popped back this morning, on the way to another project, to check how it held up overnight with the sluice gates open and water flowing through the channel."

Keya had no idea what might have frightened Rowan, but she climbed into her car and drove to Coln Akeman, instead of Cirencester.

A number of vehicles were already in the car park and as she walked across to the antiques centre, Keya noticed that the door of the auction house was open.

Had the sighting of a woman matching Tasha's description the previous day been a hoax, just as Inspector Evans had feared?

She entered the antiques centre. Only the lights at the front illuminated the large space and as she walked towards the cafe area, the empty stalls felt eerie in the gloom. The hair on the back of her neck prickled.

She found Gilly in the empty cafe space, trying to calm an agitated Rowan.

"It was the weeping widow ghost, floating on the water, I'm sure," insisted Rowan.

As Keya joined them, she asked, "Where did you see it?"

"In the river, beside the sluice gates."

Why would a ghost be bobbing against those? wondered Keya. "What did it look like?" she asked.

"It was white, of course. Her dress was spread out on the water and her dark hair framed around her like a halo."

That was a very specific description.

"And when was this?"

"About forty minutes ago. I was standing on the wall of the channel, watching the waterwheel when I spotted her. It was such a shock, I nearly fell off."

Keya remembered she had fallen off the wall that divided the river from the waterwheel channel the previous month.

"And then she floated past me in the river."

"She what?" cried Keya, no longer thinking about her own clumsiness.

"She floated down the river," repeated Rowan.

Keya felt a chill, as if she was back in the river water.

"Stay here," she commanded and ran out of the old mill and across the building site to the back of the auction house. Slowing to a jog, she continued along the side of the building, arriving at the front door puffing.

Inspector Sue met her and, as she placed her car keys in her bag, she asked in a sharp tone, "What's happened?"

"I think Tasha's in the river."

"Chief Inspector Greg has drawn a similar conclusion, but why the rush?" asked Inspector Sue.

"Because I think one of the builders saw her body float past about half an hour ago."

Businesslike, Inspector Sue said, "We need to find her. She might still be alive." She turned back through the front door and Keya followed her through reception and into the main auction room.

Chief Inspector Greg was in the middle of a briefing. It looked like his whole team was sitting or standing facing the raised stage he was speaking from.

"So next we …" The chief inspector stopped and looked quizzically at Inspector Sue, who nodded.

"Give me a minute," said Chief Inspector Greg as he jumped off the stage and strode across to join Keya and Inspector Sue.

"News?" he asked.

"You tell him," said Inspector Sue.

Keya recounted what Rowan had told her.

"You're right. That could be Natasha, either dead or alive. Let's hope it's the latter, and not this ghost everyone is obsessed with."

The inspector turned back to his team and clapped his hands for silence.

"We've had a possible sighting of Natasha in the river, flowing past here less than an hour ago. Mike, contact the search and rescue team. We need divers down here. Jenny and Adam, we need your teams to search the riverbanks, one on either side. Nick, come with me. We'll speak to the witness and try to persuade him not to tell his story immediately on social media."

"What about the tracker dogs?" called a male voice.

"Yes, we'd better organise those, too. This is probably our last chance to find Natasha alive."

Chief Inspector Greg took the radio a young officer handed him and turned back to Keya. "Take me to your witness."

Keya led the chief inspector, Inspector Sue, and Nick back across the building site to the waterwheel, where the tall willowy figure of Rowan was waiting for them. Gilly must have returned to the antiques centre.

When they reached Rowan, Keya introduced the other police officers before asking, "Can you repeat what you said to me about the figure in the water?"

"You mean the ghost?" Rowan repeated his story.

By the time he'd finished, a group of police officers had gathered on the riverbank by the stone bridge which led to the waterwheel channel wall.

They were all wearing dark waterproof trousers, bright yellow jackets, and small red life jackets. White hard hats protected their heads, and they were all carrying long yellow poles. They looked professional and serious.

"Jenny," the chief inspector called. "Start there and work your way downstream."

Two of the group clambered into the water while the rest searched the riverbank.

The chief inspector's radio crackled, and he spoke to Adam, the leader of the other team, who Keya could see standing precariously on the far river back, between the trees. Nobody climbed into the water, which Keya suspected was deep at that point, but they used their yellow poles to poke at the tree roots and undergrowth at the river's edge.

Nick had taken Rowan to one side, and they were talking earnestly.

"What do you want me to do?" Inspector Sue asked.

"You better return to the hotel and speak to the family. It won't take long for a passer-by to notice our activity in the river and to put two and two together and make five. Speak to the comms team before you leave and ask them to keep you updated. Now, I need somewhere to oversee the search."

"The bridge makes a good vantage point," Keya suggested.

"Yes, and come with me. I need you here in case we don't find Natasha alive."

Keya led the chief inspector to the stone bridge which spanned the River Coln. The road which crossed it linked Coln Akeman with the main road into Cirencester. Every so often, the chief inspector stopped and spoke into his radio.

Once on top of the bridge, they could clearly see Jenny's team on the Coln Akeman side of the river, and they were making good progress. The other team continued to be hampered by trees and thick undergrowth.

As the chief inspector spoke to Jenny again, Keya walked further down the bridge and called Inspector Evans.

"I thought we agreed you'd come to the station this morning," the inspector said by way of a greeting.

"Yes, sir. That was until I had a call about something strange at Akemans."

"What now?" groaned the inspector.

"One of the building contractors might have seen Tasha Nkosi in the river."

"Really?" The inspector suddenly sounded alert.

"Chief Inspector Greg already has two teams searching the riverbanks, and he's called in divers and tracker dogs."

"It sounds like he's throwing all his resources at this."

"Yes, sir. I think it's his final push."

"Thank you for informing me, Sergeant. It's quiet here, so I'll send

PC Jenkins to join you, in case this changes from a missing person to an unknown death case."

"Yes, sir."

For another hour, Keya shadowed Chief Inspector Greg. Ryan joined them on the bridge, looking alert and interested. They watched another team back a trailer along the fence line of Akeman's building site down to the river and launch a black inflatable boat into the water.

Two men wearing oxygen tanks and diving equipment joined the boat's life-jacketed driver and they sped down the river until they were parallel with the search teams on the riverbanks.

The team on the far bank had caught up when the wood had opened up to grass fields, while the group on the near bank had slowed down to search an area of thick reeds.

Keya was just wondering whether she and Ryan should head back to the police station when Chief Inspector Greg's radio crackled. Adam, leader of the team on the far bank, said, "Sir, we've found her."

The chief inspector, Keya and Ryan all looked toward Adam's team, who were gathered at a bend in the river, beside a fallen tree whose trunk and branches reached into the water.

Keya held her breath.

"I'm afraid she's dead, sir," Adam said over the radio.

Keya's heart clenched. Oh no! Even after all this time, and all the searching, she really thought they'd find Tasha alive.

Ryan gave her a sympathetic smile and as she looked down the river she could tell from the hunched posture of the divers in the boat, and the shaking of heads from Jenny's group, just how devastating this news was for all the chief inspector's team.

The boat engine roared into life as the driver steered it towards the fallen tree.

Chief Inspector Greg walked across the bridge, and Keya and Ryan looked at each other.

"I'll join you in a minute," said Ryan, removing his phone.

"Who are you calling?"

"Ozzie."

"Really?"

"We can't stop this story breaking and I'd rather have Ozzie telling the truth than other papers sensationalising the situation. Besides, she did give us that tip off, and this is her big break."

So Ryan knew why Ozzie had wanted to contact her on Saturday morning.

"I suppose you're right," conceded Keya. "But call Inspector Evans first, and when you're finished, join me and the chief inspector on the riverbank. A dead body means this is now our case."

CHAPTER TWENTY-NINE

Keya followed the path Chief Inspector Greg had taken across the grass field on the far bank of the River Coln.

She arrived as the divers, who were no longer in the boat, swam to the body, which was face down.

"It is Tasha, isn't it?" she asked, although if it wasn't, they had another dead woman on their hands.

"I'm afraid so," confirmed Chief Inspector Greg, staring at the water.

"Shouldn't we wait for the SOCO team? Moving the body might damage any forensic evidence."

The chief inspector turned to her and replied, "The boys and I are used to such cases, unfortunately. It's better to move the body to the boat and place it inside a body bag, rather than risk losing it down the river."

That was a fair point, conceded Keya.

"The water will already have washed the body clean, but we'll take samples of water from here, and the boys will be as careful as they can lifting her out of the water."

As one of the divers snapped the twigs off the branches that held Tasha's body in place and she moved gently in the water, Keya thought how ethereal she looked in her white tunic top over white pyjama or trouser bottoms.

Ryan joined the group and announced, "Inspector Evans will call the SOCO team from Cheltenham and stress the importance of this high-profile case. Then he'll join us."

Chief Inspector Greg mused, "Perhaps there's some advantage to only investigating cases when someone is already dead. Failure is not a life or death situation."

Keya thought he meant unlike missing person cases.

"That's not always true. If someone has killed once, they may try again unless we stop them."

Ryan cleared his throat.

"Yes, Constable," said the chief inspector. Keya could tell he was trying to gather his thoughts and put aside his personal feelings.

"Do we have any idea how long Tasha has been in the water?" Ryan asked.

Chief Inspector Greg looked at the diver closest to the bank who was guiding Tasha's head, while the other diver pulled at her feet. The diver held up three fingers.

"At least three days. When a body falls into the water it sinks to the bottom. These rivers are scattered with debris. Tree branches, shopping trolleys and other discarded items which can catch or snag a body and hold it down. But as it decomposes, the body fills with gases, increasing its buoyancy, and at this point it often detaches itself from whatever it's caught up in and rises to the surface. This process takes around three days, which is why the diver held three fingers up."

"So that would make it Saturday, the day after Tasha disappeared," Ryan said.

"Not necessarily. My experience tells me that she entered the water the day she disappeared. I'm sure someone would have spotted her in or around Coln Akeman on Friday if she wasn't already in the water," explained the chief inspector.

"Poor Tasha. And what about her family?"

"I've spoken to Sue. She'll break the news to them, but I'll visit and give them my condolences as soon as I've briefed your inspector. I owe it to them."

Keya bowed her head. She understood guilt and thought hers should be deeper than the chief inspector's on this occasion. If he was right, by the time his team arrived, Tasha was already dead. She was the only one who could have stopped this.

She felt a hand squeeze her shoulder. "I recognise that stance, and if you're feeling guilty for not preventing her death, please don't," Chief Inspector Greg consoled her.

"We have no idea what happened, or who else was involved. And if Natasha decided to take her own life, there was little you could do to stop her."

Keya lifted her head and smiled weakly at the chief inspector.

He nodded back.

They both understood the responsibility of their positions, and the guilt of failure.

"All done," shouted the driver of the boat.

Chief Inspector Greg raised a hand, and the boat slipped away through the water back towards Akemans.

"I'll check in with my search teams and meet you and your inspector back at the auction house," said the chief inspector. He turned and walked back along the river to the police search team, who were poking about in the plants growing at the side of the river.

"Come on," Keya said to Ryan. "We should meet the inspector."

As they wandered back across the field, Keya said, "I spoke to Dan this morning. He admitted he lied to Chief Inspector Greg's team, and he did see Tasha on Thursday night. And he knew about Tasha's pregnancy. She opened up to him after she ran off from the pub last week."

Keya repeated the rest of her conversation with Dan.

"So we've filled in some of her history, but we still don't know who she argued with the day before she disappeared."

"You mean as well as her brother?"

"Her brother?" queried Ryan.

"Didn't you read Ozzie's article?"

Ryan looked down at the footpath as they walked across the stone bridge, the River Coln flowing steadily beneath them. "She sent me the link at the weekend, but I forgot to read it."

"I suggest you do, and then call her and ask which neighbour identified Tasha's brother as a visitor on Friday afternoon, as we need to speak to them."

Keya and Ryan waited on the riverbank, behind Akemans auction house, with the boat crew. They hauled their boat onto the bank but left Tasha's body in it.

Ryan read Ozzie's article on his phone. "This is well written and very balanced. I'll call her now."

As Ryan stepped away, Keya heard Inspector Evans' Welsh baritone voice, and she turned towards the auction building. He was speaking to Sebastian, the senior SOCO officer, who was directing a reversing van.

"This is an unpleasant business, but not unexpected," Inspector Evans said when he joined Keya. He wore his customary brown suit, and Keya noticed a dark stain on his matching tie.

"But did she decide to end her own life? Or did someone help her?" the inspector mused out loud.

"We're not sure, sir. Both Ryan and I have continued to collect evidence, as you directed, but there's nothing conclusive."

The van reversed past them, blocking their view of the boat.

"Let's leave SOCO to do their job and catch up with Chief Inspector Greg. Constable," the inspector called across to Ryan, who finished his call.

When Keya, Ryan and the inspector entered the auction room, it was clear Chief Inspector Greg had already told his team the bad news. Several of the female members were in tears or hugging each other, and one of the younger men in Nick's media team was dabbing at his eyes with a tissue.

"Inspector Evans and his team from Cirencester will now take over the case, and I hope you'll assist them in every way possible to find out what happened to Natasha."

Inspector Evans strode towards the stage while Keya and Ryan hung back.

"Thank you, Chief Inspector." Inspector Evans turned towards the room. "I know how hard you've worked on this case, and this is the worst possible outcome. But I promise you, my team and I will work tirelessly and diligently to establish what happened. And if another party is involved, we'll bring them to justice."

He turned back to the chief inspector and asked, "Perhaps you could brief your team a final time, and we can sit in and ask questions."

Different sections of Chief Inspector Greg's team gave their updates.

"Who searched the village?" asked Inspector Evans, after an older man spoke about the extensive searches conducted on Friday evening and Saturday.

"On Friday, most of us here, but Saturday's search concentrated on the less accessible areas around the village," replied the police officer.

"And had anyone seen Miss Nkosi since she returned from Cirencester on Thursday evening?"

The policeman shook his head.

Keya cleared her throat. "Daniel Hirst did."

"When?" asked the chief inspector sharply.

"Late. After he and Tasha exchanged text messages when she returned from her meal in Cirencester."

"But he told us he hadn't visited her." Chief Inspector Greg's eyes narrowed.

"I know. He admitted to me that he lied, but he was there."

"When we've finished here, bring him to the station for questioning," directed Inspector Evans.

"Yes, sir." Keya knew Dan wouldn't want that, but they had to be meticulous in their investigation as their actions would be under scrutiny from the press and divisional police headquarters. But more importantly, they needed to do things right for Tasha's family.

Inspector Evans concluded, "Let's crack this case."

CHAPTER THIRTY

Keya, Ryan and Inspector Evans left Nick at Akemans packing up equipment with the rest of Chief Inspector Greg's team.

Keya was relieved to enter the familiar bustle of Cirencester Police station. She and Ryan sat down at their desks, and she'd just switched on her computer when Stan Rowbottom entered carrying two cups of tea and clutching a Tupperware container under his arm.

Stan had been a long-standing sergeant in the station until he'd been offered early retirement. He'd taken it, but on the condition he could continue working at the station in charge of the archives.

He was a pleasant 'old timer' as some members of the station referred to him, but his knowledge of past cases came in handy. He also liked to help out where he could on current ones.

"I thought you might be hungry and thirsty after the disappointing news today."

"Which travels fast," Keya observed.

"Didn't you see Sergeant Onion sitting alongside Chief Inspector Foster for the press conference? I must say, they both looked very sombre as they spoke about the discovery of that young lass's body. Is it true the only sign of her being near the river is her gold necklace?"

"Yes," Keya replied as she turned to Ryan. "Did we bring it back with us?"

"I don't have it," Ryan replied.

"Don't worry, I've signed for it," said Inspector Evans, entering the room. "Lovely, tea." He picked up the cup on Ryan's desk.

Ryan clenched his jaw, a barely perceptible movement before his face relaxed, and he asked, "Sergeant Varma asked earlier if the chain was snapped, sir. Is it?"

"No," replied the inspector. "The chief inspector's team found it intact, laid on a bench beside the river."

"I wonder if it's a sign. If she meant it to tell us something. Ezra, her fiancé, gave her the heart and chain," said Keya.

"That's for you to find out," directed the inspector. "As to the cause of death, Sebastian was his usual negative self and said it could be several days before they know. He complained that the time she spent in the water makes his team's job much harder. But that's what they're paid to do."

Keya considered the inspector. His mood was particularly belligerent today. Was that because Tasha had turned up dead?

"Are those sandwiches, Stan?" asked the inspector, staring at the Tupperware box.

"Yes, my missus always makes more than I need, and I thought your team might have missed lunch, with the dead girl and that..."

"We have and I am," replied the inspector.

Stan opened the box and said, "The white bread ones are egg. You might prefer ham and mustard, in the brown bread."

"Thank you," said the inspector, taking two brown bread sandwiches in his large hand. He carried them and the cup of tea into his office.

Stan shrugged his shoulders apologetically as Ryan took a sandwich and he then offered the container to Keya, who removed an egg sandwich.

"Thanks, Stan. I think everyone is upset about the outcome of this case."

"I suppose you're right. I'll make you another cup of tea, Ryan." Stan took his depleted container of sandwiches and left the room.

Inspector Evans walked back into the team room and asked, "Shouldn't you two be elsewhere?"

Ryan pushed back his chair and jumped up. "Yes, sir. Where?"

Keya finished her mouthful of sandwich before replying. "Daniel Hirst is working on a project in Cirencester at the moment. Shall we question him on site or bring him back here?"

"Let's keep this low-key but official," replied the inspector. "Bring him back here, but you and PC Jenkins interview him."

Stan returned and passed Ryan a mug of tea.

Inspector Evans nodded and said, "Finish your lunch first. Miss Nkosi has been dead for several days, so a few more minutes won't make any difference." He retired to his office and closed the door.

"Was that an apology?" asked Ryan.

"As close as," Stan replied. "Now, what do you need me to do?"

Keya and Ryan walked down Market Place in the centre of Cirencester. The pleasant June sun shone on the two and three-storey pastel-coloured buildings.

Shoppers wearing shorts and sundresses were ambling slowly along the pavement or sitting at one of the many tables which sprang up outside cafes and restaurants in the summer.

"I'm still hungry," moaned Ryan.

"Do you want to stop somewhere and pick up a sandwich or a slice of cake?"

Ryan wrinkled his nose. "No, I probably won't get the chance to eat it."

They passed the grand, gothic style, stone entrance building of St John Baptist Church and turned right. Keya glanced at the bench behind the church, and the park beyond, where she used to sit during her lunch breaks. She no longer had time to just sit and observe the world pass by.

She said, "I found out from Vic, the cafe site manager, that the project Dan is working on is down Black Jack Street."

They turned left and entered a narrow one-way street with two and three-storey stone buildings on either side, which blocked out the sun.

"I think this is the one," Keya said. They were standing outside a stone building which had a large stone entrance and standard windows instead of the usual glass shop front.

They heard drilling and banging, so they stepped inside. The man drilling a hole in the wall near them stopped and looked over. He asked, "Is the clothes shop next door complaining about the noise again? I've told them, the more they complain, the longer this will take us."

"No, we're here to see Dan," Keya replied.

"He's upstairs. I'll radio him."

He picked up a small walkie-talkie and said, "Dan, two police officers are downstairs to see you."

Dan didn't appear to reply, but a minute late rushed into the room. "Keya, is it Tasha? Have you found her?"

Keya hadn't expected to break the bad news to Dan. She stepped forward and in an apologetic voice said, "I'm sorry, but we found her body in the river this morning."

Dan leaned against an exposed stone wall, gasping for air.

"I know this is a shock," said Keya. "And upsetting. But for Tasha's sake, we need you to come back to the station with us and make a formal statement."

"Do you know how she died?" Dan asked, his face paler than the honey-coloured stone of the wall behind him.

"I'm afraid not, so for now, we are treating it as a suspicious death."

"Am I a suspect?"

Ryan stepped forward and answered, "We need to take statements from everyone who has been in contact with her recently."

"Yes, of course. Let me just give the boys upstairs their instructions."

Ryan looked at Keya.

She said, "Dan, we can't let you do that. Police procedure and everything. We need you to come with us now."

Dan turned to the man with the drill, who'd listened to the entire conversation. "We need to fit the lighting above the upstairs bar, and then start in the restaurant area."

The man nodded, put down his drill and walked away as Keya, Ryan, and Dan left the building.

CHAPTER THIRTY-ONE

Dan sat on the far side of a grey Formica table in a grey-painted interview room at Cirencester Police Station. His puffy red eyes betrayed his feelings over Tasha's death.

He dabbed his nose with a tissue and thanked Ryan, who placed a cup of tea in front of him.

Ryan sat down next to Keya and tapped the recording equipment before nodding at Keya, who said, "Present are Sergeant Keya Varma."

"Constable Ryan Jenkins," said Ryan.

Keya nodded her head at Dan, who said, "Daniel Hirst."

In a friendly tone, Keya said, "Tell us how you first met Tasha."

Dan replied, "It was at college." He spoke about the interior design module they took together, the projects they worked on and their growing friendship.

"But I had a work placement and by the time I returned to finish my course, Tasha had returned to London."

"And did you keep in contact?" Keya asked.

"Not really," Dan shook his head. "Occasionally I'd see something I'd think she'd find funny and send it to her, but her delay responding grew and, in the end, I gave up. But I followed her social media posts and occasionally commented. I was so proud when her modelling took off and she became the face of Farmers Jewellery. It was a shock when she and Ezra announced their engagement, but he was from a rich, successful family and I hoped she'd be happy."

"I have to ask," Keya said in an apologetic tone. "Were you jealous?"

Dan squished his lips together. "Not jealous, but a little sad. It wasn't as if anything had ever happened between us. We were just friends. But would I have liked there to be more? In a perfect world, yes. But in this one, she has always been out of my league, and I don't think her parents' idea of a husband is a humble shop-fitter."

"Why do you say that?" asked Ryan.

"Just the impression she gave. And the odd comment she dropped about her father, and his view of life." Dan stopped and looked down at his cooling mug of tea.

"What are you thinking?" asked Keya.

Dan looked up and his eyes glistened. "That I should have seen the signs, even then. The burden that her family was placing on her, and their expectations of her."

"Are you saying this is her father's fault?" asked Keya.

"What I'm saying," replied Dan, "is that she has always had to live her life as her father wanted her to. That she was expected to act in whatever way was best for the family."

"You mean marry well and bring them prestige and wealth?" queried Keya.

"Exactly, and not just the marriage. Modelling helped achieve that, although we know the consequences of it."

Keya nodded. "The parties, and ultimately the pregnancy."

"She knew how upset her father would be, which is why she didn't tell him."

"Back to you, Dan," said Keya. "When did Tasha get in touch with you?"

"She sent me a message and said she'd moved into a cottage in Coln Akeman and was preparing for her wedding, and that it would be nice to catch up."

"Was that night we were in The Axeman the first time you'd seen Tasha since she'd moved to the Cotswolds?"

Dan hesitated.

"Clearly not," observed Keya. "Did you meet her at the pub or cottage before that? How many times had you seen her?"

"Tasha had been in Coln Akeman for a month by the time we had that drink with you at The Axeman, and I'd seen her half a dozen times. But I was worried. To start with she slept a lot, but then I persuaded her to go for walks. I also brought food and cooked meals, as she was wasting away."

"The two of you were growing close?"

"Yes, but not in the way you think." Dan held Keya's gaze.

Keya remained silent.

"I met Ezra, and I could see how much he cared for her. And I also knew he was worried about Tasha." Dan looked down at the tabletop and placed his hands around his cup.

Keya waited.

Dan looked up at Keya and then at Ryan. It was clear he was battling to keep his feelings under control. In a strained voice, he said, "There was never anything romantic about our relationship. However much I wanted to kiss Tasha, I didn't, as I respected her and the choices she made." He leaned back. "She wasn't stupid. She knew how I felt, which I think is why she trusted me."

Dan gulped. "I didn't do anything to harm Tasha."

Keya and Ryan watched Dan as he drew his lips together and wiped away a tear that dropped onto his chin. Keya wanted to believe him, but she also needed to find out the truth.

"Who did Tasha argue with the day before she went missing?"

Dan clamped his lips tighter into a narrow line.

"Why did you visit her so late on Thursday night? Who had upset her?"

Dan crossed his arms.

Keya realised she'd lost him. But when? And why? What was he hiding? And who was he protecting?

CHAPTER THIRTY-TWO

Keya and Ryan left the uncommunicative Dan in the interview room and returned to their team room, where Keya summarised their interview for Inspector Evans.

"And that's it? He clammed up." Inspector Evans' eyebrows drew together.

"Yes, sir," replied Keya.

"What's he hiding?"

"I'm not sure, but there's definitely something he's not telling us. Do you want to interview him?"

"I'm not sure he'll be any more forthcoming with me. We need to do some digging. Chief Inspector Greg is coming over with Sergeant Unwin, so I'll see if he has anything to add. Why don't you two interview Miss Nkosi's family while Inspector Honeywell is still with them? I'll call and let her know you're on your way."

"And Dan?"

"I'll speak to the custody sergeant and either move him to a holding cell or leave him where he is."

Keya and Ryan collected their radios and left the station. They climbed into Keya's official police Ford Focus and as Keya drove out of Cirencester, Ryan's phone rang.

"Hi, Ozzie," he said hesitantly and then listened for a reply. "Oh, good, because I can't tell you anything."

He listened again. "Of course. Thanks for calling me back. It was about the source of your newspaper article. Who told you they saw those men visit our victim?"

"The deaf one?" Ryan listened for another minute before finishing the call.

He said to Keya, "It wasn't a neighbour Ozzie spoke to but the daughter of the deaf lady who lives next door to Rose Cottage. Apparently, she visits once a day. I'm not sure who she or her mother saw, but Ozzie's called her and she's with her mother at Coln Akeman at the moment. Understandably, her mother is upset by all the reporters hanging around asking questions every time she leaves the house."

Keya was lucky to find a parking space by the village green in Coln Akeman. If anything, the number of outdoor broadcasting vehicles had increased.

Groups of television reporters were scattered across the green. Some only had one camera operator with them, while others were surrounded by four or five technicians.

Someone spotted Ryan and Keya striding along the path beside the green and pointed towards them. Keya picked up her speed as other reporters noticed their arrival. As Keya and Ryan approached Rose Cottage, the reporters moved in and the questions started.

"How did Natasha die?"

"Was anyone else involved?"

"Have you identified the cause of death?"

Keya spotted Otto standing beside the gate of the neighbouring cottage which they were visiting. His phone was once again attached to the black metal stick, and she presumed he was filming their approach.

Keya walked past Rose Cottage and approached Otto.

"You don't suspect Mrs Angles, do you?" asked Otto, his eyes widening.

Keya tilted her head at him.

"Oh, she's a witness."

As Keya walked down the garden path, she heard a reporter ask, "Who's Mrs Angles?"

She glanced back at Ryan, who was closing the small white wooden gate. Beyond him Otto was preening as he answered the reporter's question, with cameras and microphones turned towards him. Keya couldn't help smiling to herself. This was Otto's five minutes of fame.

The front door opened before Keya had a chance to knock and a young woman with mousey blonde hair ushered them inside.

"Can't you tell them to go away?" asked the woman. "They're upsetting mother."

"I'm afraid not," replied Keya, "but now Miss Nkosi has been found, their interest in the village will wane."

"Until that ghost shows up again." The woman's lips pressed together in irritation.

Ryan smiled sympathetically and asked, "Have there been any recent sightings?"

"What's that? Have we had any fighting?" said an elderly lady leaning on a walking stick. "There will be if they stop me going out for my morning walk again."

The younger woman looked at Keya and rolled her eyes. She turned back to the elderly lady, who Keya presumed was Mrs Angles, and said slowly and clearly, "Mother, these police officers have come to ask us about Natasha, who lived next door."

"Nice girl. Helped me find my glasses." Mrs Angles turned and hobbled back into a small living room with chintzy armchairs. She sat down in a high-backed armchair and waved her stick at the others. "Sit down," she directed. "Molly will make us tea."

As Keya sat down, she said, "Thank you, but we're fine. How well did you know Natasha?"

"Well? I'm a bit deaf, though. Natasha didn't live here long. But it was nice not having weekenders with loud parties or wailing children, like during the holidays. I didn't speak to Natasha much, did you, Molly?"

Molly approached her mother's chair and shook her head. "No, we exchanged pleasantries about the weather, but that was all."

"What's happened to my shawl?" asked Mrs Angles indignantly.

"Molly squatted down beside her mother's chair. "Are you cold? Would you like me to find it?"

"I don't need it now. Stop fussing. But did Natasha give it back?"

"I don't know." Molly frowned and stood up.

"We'll look in Rose Cottage," assured Keya. "When did you give it to her?"

"I only lent it. She was always wandering out in the evening in her pyjamas. I told her to wear my shawl so she wouldn't catch her death."

Ryan coughed, but Mrs Angles seemed oblivious to her choice of words.

The older lady shook her head. "A pretty young girl like that shouldn't be so sad."

"Why did you think she was sad?" Keya enquired.

Mrs Angles bristled. "I might be deaf, but I'm not senile. I could tell she was unhappy."

"And last Thursday, did you see her brother, Nate?"

"Late? Late for what?" asked the older woman.

"No mother," said Molly, "nobody's late." She looked at Keya and Ryan and said, "Actually, I was the one who saw her brother. It was the day before Natasha disappeared and he didn't look at all happy when he left. I'd heard them arguing earlier when I brought in mother's washing."

"What was Natasha doing with my washing?"

"Nothing, Mother."

"And is Nate the only visitor you've seen?"

"I've seen her attractive fiancé. He always smiles at me." Molly's cheeks flushed.

"Don't be silly, girl," chided Mrs Angles. "You'd be better off with the other young man."

"Which man? Nate or Dan?" queried Keya.

"Dan. He was also pleasant and chatted with me when he visited Natasha. I saw him a few times and sometimes he even brought Natasha groceries."

Mrs Angles nodded in approval. "Shame her family couldn't do that."

"They live in London," Keya said.

"Doesn't stop her father visiting."

Keya sat up. "When has he visited?"

"He's come two or three times," said Mrs Angles. "The last time was, let me see... The day before I found her front door open."

"You saw Tasha's father visit her cottage the day before she disappeared?" Keya clarified.

"You didn't tell me," said Molly, sounding put out.

"I don't tell you everything, girl. Besides, why shouldn't a father visit his daughter?"

"What time was this?" asked Keya.

"Late. The security light next door came on as I was closing my bedroom curtain and I saw him walk up the garden path."

"Did you see him leave?"

Mrs Angles shook her head.

Keya asked Mrs Angles and Molly a few additional questions, but they had nothing more to add.

"Thank you for your help," Keya said, standing up.

Mrs Angles waved her stick. "Go out the back, into the lane. There'll be fewer reporters there."

The old lady was right. The lane running along the back of the cottages was clear of reporters, and Keya and Ryan reached her car without being questioned and drove off.

Coln St Aldwyns was even prettier and more photogenic than Coln Akeman with the River Coln, an attractive church with a stone tower, and rows of cottages built of Cotswold stone.

She found The Manor House Hotel on the far side of the village, in what she imagined was once a large manor house, just as the name suggested.

A not particularly attractive two-storey extension, visible from the entrance to the drive, extended back from the main period building, with rows of windows which Keya presumed were some of the hotel's bedrooms.

"I thought there would be reporters here," Ryan said.

"I'd like to think they have the decency to give the family space, but they seem to be concentrating on Coln Akeman for the moment."

"Let's hope it stays that way," muttered Ryan.

Keya parked in a visitors' parking space and Ryan ducked his head as they entered the hotel through a stone entrance.

Inspector Sue rose from a tartan-covered armchair and smiled sadly at them. "Inspector Evans called and told me it's important you speak to Natasha's family. But I hope you'll be considerate. The news of her death has been a huge shock."

"Of course," Keya agreed.

"Perhaps you could speak to Nate first and give Solomon and Linda more time to compose themselves."

Keya hesitated. She didn't want to give Tasha's parents time to make up a story, but would they really do that? The case must be getting to her if she was starting to think the worst of everyone.

"Yes, we can start with Nate. Where do you suggest we speak to him?" asked Keya.

"I've secured the use of the hotel's small function room. It's rather stark, but you won't be disturbed."

Inspector Sue turned and led them down a corridor before opening a brown door on the right.

Metal chairs with blue seats were stacked against one wall, but a square wooden table and six of the chairs had been positioned in the middle of the room. A jug of water and a tray of glasses had been placed on the table.

Inspector Sue said, "I'll fetch Nate."

CHAPTER THIRTY-THREE

The door of the hotel's function room opened, and Keya looked up expecting to see Nate. Instead, a young woman who in some many ways resembled Tasha, although she was much shorter, walked in.

Ryan turned towards the door and gasped.

The woman stopped several paces away from the table and ran her hands nervously down the front of her pale cream tailored trousers.

"Are you Naomi?" Keya asked.

"Yes, I'm Tasha's sister and I needed to speak to you, as I've just arrived from London and I can't believe my sister is dead." The finality of the word 'dead,' seemed to halt her outpouring and her olive-coloured skin, so similar to her sister's, paled.

"Come and sit down," suggested Keya. "We don't bite. I'm Sergeant Varma and this is my colleague, Constable Jenkins. My sister and I met with Tasha last week."

Naomi nodded as she pulled out a chair and sat down. "Tasha told me all about your sister's wedding venue mix-up. She really wanted to cancel her wedding so your sister's could take place, and run away with Ezra and marry him on a Caribbean island. She'd have looked beautiful on a white sandy beach."

Keya thought Tasha would have looked beautiful anywhere, particularly if she was happy and smiling.

"I even offered to buy her a ticket so Dad wouldn't find out, but she said Ezra wouldn't go as he didn't want to let his family down after all the effort they'd put into organising the wedding."

Now for the difficult question, thought Keya, and she maintained a sympathetic expression as she said, "You were obviously close to your sister. Why didn't you come down to help her? To support her?"

Naomi clasped her hands together on the top of the table. "I tried to, but I needed to finish a project at work before I could travel down, and the client kept changing the report they needed. We had long chats on the phone and spoke about growing up and holidays and the things we'd done, and she always seemed more upbeat by the end of our calls."

Keya couldn't help wondering how much Naomi could have helped her sister if she'd actually visited and talked to her in person.

"Please don't judge me," pleaded Naomi. "I feel terrible that I wasn't here to help Tasha. But do you know what happened to her? Sue won't tell us anything."

"That's because she doesn't know," conceded Keya. "None of us do at the moment, I'm afraid. Which is why PC Jenkins and I are trying to establish what Tasha did, and who she saw or spoke to before she … disappeared."

Naomi squinted and seemed to be considering Keya's words.

Ryan cleared his throat and said, "Tasha was a successful model, and she led a colourful life in London. But do you know if anyone had been threatening her? Were there any reasons apart from the wedding that she moved out to the Cotswolds?"

"I don't know that her modelling was that successful. She was only a photographic model. Not one who strutted down catwalks. Sure, she enjoyed it. The glamour and the parties, but it was always secondary to her day job in marketing."

Naomi tilted her head and added, "I suppose she had been doing more photo shoots recently, and attending more high-profile parties. But she wasn't into drugs, if that's what you're getting at." She crossed her arms.

In a calm voice, Keya said, "We're not getting at anything, apart from the truth. And to find that we have to understand more about Tasha's life in general. So you don't know of any other reason, apart from the wedding, that Tasha was living alone in the Cotswolds."

Naomi lifted her head and jutted out her chin. "None," she said definitely.

"Not even the loss of her baby?" Keya's voice was quiet and even.

Naomi's mouth opened and then closed again.

"We know about it, and the devastating affect it had on your sister. But we do need to know if anything else was upsetting her. Or anyone," Keya pushed.

Naomi remained silent.

"Like your brother?" suggested Ryan.

Naomi narrowed her eyes. "What did Nate do?"

"We have a witness who saw him visit Tasha the day before she disappeared. And this witness heard arguing and saw your brother storm out."

"Typical!"

"What's typical?"

"Nate badgering Tasha. He's always tried to use her success, and her contacts, to his advantage. Even her marriage."

"Is that why they were arguing?"

"I expect so. I think he had some sort of deal going on with the Farmers. If Tasha was thinking of postponing the wedding, which I'm not saying she was, then it might have upset Nate's plans. Or it might just be she found out about them."

"So your brother was benefiting from your sister's marriage to Ezra Farmer?" Keya clarified.

"That's about the long and the short of it, and I wouldn't be surprised if he wasn't the only one."

"What do you mean?" asked Keya.

"Nothing." Naomi sprang to her feet. "I need to see how Mum is." She hurriedly left the room.

"What was all that about?" asked Ryan.

"I'm not sure, but the inspector told us to start digging and I think he was right. There's more to find here than just a grieving family."

There was a knock at the door and Inspector Sue entered. "I'm sorry, but I can't find Nate, and Solomon has just admitted that his car keys are missing."

"Does he think Nate has taken them?" asked Keya.

"That's the obvious answer."

Before Keya could respond, there was a gentle tap on the open door.

Inspector Sue turned round and proclaimed, "Linda!"

"I wondered if I might have a quick word with your colleagues. I've just seen Naomi, and she's rather upset. I've persuaded her to take Solomon for a walk. I can't go far at the moment as my hip's bothering me."

Sue turned and looked at Keya, who nodded.

As Linda hobbled forward, it was clear her hip was causing her pain.

"I'll be in reception if you need me," said Inspector Sue before she left, closing the door behind her.

Linda sat down and said apologetically, "I'm sorry to bother you, but, well ..."

"Mrs Nkosi," said Keya. "I appreciate you wanting to speak to us, and all we're trying to do is find out what happened to your daughter."

Linda nodded. "I appreciate that, and I know you were one of the few people who tried to help Tasha."

Linda looked down at her lap and mumbled, "I didn't."

Keya leaned forward and said in a compassionate tone, "I'm sure you did what you could."

'But did I?" Linda looked up, and a tear glinted on her cheek. "I knew the pressure Solomon was putting on Tasha with this wedding. You see, to him she's always been his princess."

Linda stopped and reached across the table for a glass.

Keya poured water from the jug into one and slid it towards Linda.

Linda sipped her water before continuing. "My husband is a proud man, and in many ways old-fashioned. Tasha was his favourite, and, in his eyes, she could do no wrong. But she was a young, independent woman who needed to experience life. Solomon didn't see it that way and thought she should stay at home until he found her the perfect husband."

She sipped her water again. "I was surprised he approved of the modelling, but he accompanied her to start with and probably appreciated the admiration others had for Tasha. She was wonderfully photogenic. And then she became the face of Farmers Jewellers, a respectable family firm which Solomon approved of. And the attention of their son and heir was the icing on the cake. All Solomon's hopes and dreams for his favourite child were coming true."

"So what went wrong?" asked Keya, although she thought she knew.

"Tasha rebelled. Not in a huge way. It started because she simply wanted to go out with her friends and colleagues after some of her modelling sessions. But Solomon tried to stop her. She went anyway, which made him furious, so she partied even more. She confided in me that she hated being at home with Solomon's brooding disapproval. And I'm sure by now you know what happened. The pregnancy and the miscarriage. My poor baby."

Linda glanced down and, mesmerised, Keya watched a tear fall to her lap. But why hadn't Linda intervened?

"How did you help her?" asked Keya, trying not to sound judgmental.

"I … it was so difficult. Call me old-fashioned, but I grew up to respect my husband and follow his rules. I did comfort Tasha, but when she asked me to speak to her father, I did let her down. What could I say to make Solomon change his mind?"

"Did you feel you had to choose between your husband and your daughter?" Keya asked. It was a common occurrence among Indian families she knew, where daughters wanted to follow the same path in life as their non-Indian friends.

Linda nodded.

"Did Solomon know about Tasha's pregnancy?"

Linda drew her lips together.

Keya looked at Ryan and they waited in silence.

Eventually Linda replied, "Not until she lost the baby. He couldn't understand why she was so upset and crying all the time and eventually she broke and admitted she'd been pregnant." Linda sipped her water again.

"He was shocked rather than angry. I honestly think he believed his beloved daughter was still pure and untouched. He never could get his head around the fact that she'd grown up into a young woman with her own needs and desires."

"So what did your husband do?" pressed Keya.

"He banished Tasha to the Cotswolds."

CHAPTER THIRTY-FOUR

Keya and Ryan sat at a table in a small function room in The Manor House Hotel and looked across a wooden table at Linda, Tasha's mum.

Linda sniffed and wiped her eyes with a handkerchief she'd removed from the pocket of her sky-blue cardigan.

"What about your son, Nate, and his relationship with his sister? Do you know why they were arguing the day before she disappeared?"

Linda clenched her jaw.

"Mrs Nkosi," prompted Keya.

Linking her hands together in her lap, Linda looked up and admitted, "He's always been jealous of Tasha. Even as a child, he'd destroy a model she'd made, or tear up a picture she brought back from school. And in a way, I can't blame him. Whatever he did, it was never good enough for Solomon. So he stopped trying to please and grew into a resentful and sly boy.

"And that boy, I'm afraid, is a tricky adult. I've no idea what he's up to now, but it wouldn't surprise me if it had something to do with either Tasha's modelling or her marriage. The trouble is, the more Nate tries to do the next big thing, the harder he falls. I think he recently asked Solomon for money for a new enterprise and, once again, his father refused to help him."

"So you don't know why he and Tasha argued?" Keya asked again.

"No, but it's likely to have involved money."

A silence fell and Keya tried to think of any more questions she needed to ask Tasha's mum.

"As Nate isn't here, will you speak to Solomon next?" Linda asked.

"Yes, we should do," Keya agreed.

"Do you mind if I sit in?"

Keya glanced at Ryan, who shrugged. She said, "I don't see why not, although if I feel he's not saying something, because you're present, I'll have to ask you to leave."

Linda nodded her acceptance.

Ryan stood up and said, "I'll find Inspector Sue and see if she knows if Naomi and Solomon are back from their walk."

Ryan left and in the silence that followed Keya asked, "What was Tasha like as a girl?"

Linda smiled and regaled her with stories of an awkward and ungainly child who was always taller than her friends. It appeared that only as a teenager did Tasha grow into her body and develop the grace, poise and beauty which led her to the modelling world.

After ten minutes, Linda ran out of stories and Keya was relieved when Ryan returned, followed by a stooping Solomon. As Solomon sat down, his appearance shocked Keya. His clothes were ruffled, and he hadn't shaved.

"We're so sorry for your loss, Mr Nkosi," Keya said.

He nodded at her words and closed his eyes.

"But we are trying to find out what happened to your daughter. When did you last see her?"

Linda reached out and placed a comforting hand on her husband's arm.

He glanced across at her and muttered, "What have I done?"

"What have you done?" asked Keya in a more forthright tone than she meant to use.

Solomon's eyes widened as he turned to look at her.

"I killed her."

Linda yanked her hand away from Solomon as if his arm had burnt her.

Keya took a deep breath before asking, "And how did you do that?"

"I pushed her to marry Ezra."

Linda murmured, "But she loved Ezra. She wanted to marry him."

Solomon glanced at her and replied, "But not with a huge wedding and lots of people she didn't know."

"Did she tell you she and Ezra wanted to elope?" asked Keya. "That she wanted to cancel the wedding and have a ceremony with just the two of them?"

Solomon bowed his head. "She asked me to speak to Mr Farmer and explain to him that she appreciated all he and his wife had done organising the wedding, but it wasn't what she wanted. And that another bride was supposed to be getting married at Charbury Castle Hotel on the same day. So we should let her have her wedding and allow Tasha and Ezra some space to arrange how and where they wanted to get married."

"But you refused?"

"Worse, I didn't listen. I was furious and called her ungrateful after all the hard work everyone was putting into the wedding."

Solomon glanced across at Linda again. "But my wife made me see last night that Tasha never asked for any of it. The grand white wedding was what I'd dreamed of, and what the Farmers wanted so they could show off to their friends and other important people."

"Do you think that if you'd spoken to Ezra's parents, you could have changed the wedding?"

Solomon shifted guiltily in his seat.

Keya narrowed her eyes. Was there something else Tasha's father was hiding?

"Did you speak to them?" she pressed.

"No, I couldn't. The wedding had to go ahead."

"Why, Solomon?" Linda asked.

He turned and gazed lovingly at her. "Because then I'd have the money for your hip operation, and you wouldn't need to wait."

Linda leaned away from her husband. "I don't understand."

Keya and Ryan kept quiet as Solomon poured out his vision of

Tasha as pure and innocent and how he believed, because he'd told her to, that Tasha had refrained from intimate relationships. He explained his culture and the re-enforcement of his church that valued virginity as a source of pride, dignity, and respect.

"You see, my reputation was built on Natasha's. And I was so certain of my view of her that I convinced Ezra's parents to pay a bride price. Enough for you to have your hip operation," he said, looking at Linda. "I couldn't ask them to cancel the wedding. And what if they then found out about the baby? Everything would be lost."

"No, Solomon, it wouldn't," replied Linda flatly. "Ezra knew about the baby. I've no idea if his parents did, but he and Tasha had agreed to keep it. Chances were it was his, anyway."

"But …" Solomon eyes widened, and he froze in horror.

Linda's voice softened as she asked, "What did you do?"

Solomon slowly shook his head. "The things I said to her. Shouted at her. Calling her stupid and selfish. That she was not only ruining her life but yours, and mine. And she didn't argue back. She just cried and said over and over again how sorry she was. She pleaded for my forgiveness, but I refused and left her alone in the cottage. That was the last time I saw or spoke to her."

Solomon hunched over and gripped his legs. His whole body shook, and his sobs were loud and pitiful.

Linda watched him and Keya felt so sorry for her as different emotions passed across her face. Shock, pity, disgust.

Keya pushed back her chair, and quietly she and Ryan left the room.

They drove back to Cirencester Police Station.

"We have a lot to tell the inspector," said Ryan as they entered the station.

"Yes, but does any of it actually tell us what happened to Tasha? I have a nagging feeling I didn't ask the right questions," said Keya wearily, worried that she'd missed something important.

"Did you ask where any of them were between midnight on Thursday and eight o'clock on Friday morning, when PC Jenkins found the front door of Miss Nkosi's cottage open and nobody at home?" asked Inspector Evans, leaning against the door frame of their team room.

"No," admitted Keya, as she approached him walking along the corridor.

"I'm sure you made a good start," consoled the inspector. "Interviewing the family in such a case is never easy. Besides, we won't know if any of them is even involved until we receive the results of the post-mortem."

Keya nodded in relief.

"Write up your reports and go home, Sergeant. We'll continue with the investigation in the morning."

"What day is tomorrow?" asked Keya, feeling that this week was merging with the previous one.

"It's still Tuesday," joked Ryan.

"Really, then tomorrow is Wednesday and … that's it. I promised my neighbour, Peggy, that I'd take her to a hospital appointment in Cheltenham in the morning."

Inspector Evans pressed his lips together.

"Don't Farmers have their main jewellery store in Cheltenham?" asked Ryan, tapping his phone. "Yes, it's on the Promenade."

"Do you think I should visit it? Ezra's unlikely to be working after what happened," Keya responded.

"It's worth a try since you're in the town," agreed Inspector Evans. "Some people find the routine of work helpful in difficult times."

CHAPTER THIRTY-FIVE

"I'm so grateful to you, Keya," said Peggy the following morning as she closed her garden gate.

"I swear Derek making hay is just an excuse not to come with me today. I don't think he likes hospitals," she admitted as she climbed into Keya's car.

"But then I guess not many older people do. Full of folk like us. It reminds us of our own mortality and our dwindling days."

Keya drove to Cheltenham. She negotiated the roundabout beside The Air Balloon pub and followed the road down the hill into the Victorian spa town.

All the time Peggy chattered on about people in the village, some she knew and others she didn't, and the pub, and local school where she'd worked for many years as a dinner lady.

As it was early, a quarter to nine, Keya found a space in the car park at the front of the hospital, opposite the grand, but tired looking stone-columned entrance. It reminded Keya of a courthouse rather than a hospital.

Peggy placed her hand on Keya's leg and said, "There's no need for you to come inside. Far too depressing with the smell of antiseptic and bleach. Why not find yourself somewhere to relax with a cup of coffee?"

Keya turned and looked at Peggy. "If you're sure you'll be OK, I need to visit a shop in the town centre."

Peggy smiled. "You do that and phone me when you're finished. I've plenty to read while I wait." She reached down for a faded green tote bag, in which Keya spotted several magazines.

She accompanied Peggy to the front door of the hospital and with Peggy's encouragement, left her and walked back to the main road. Keeping the grounds of the prestigious Cheltenham College private school on her left, she walked until she reached the traffic lights at the junction with the Bath Road.

Ten minutes later, she reached the Promenade. It was a wide street with a formal grassy area and trees running down the centre, and roads on either side.

Through the leaves, she spotted a statue of a man with a military bearing and beyond him a formal stone terrace of buildings typical of Cheltenham. She thought Dotty had told her once it was Regency architecture.

Specialist and boutique shops fronted the pavement, including high-end clothes and shoe shops and an art gallery. She found Farmers Jewellers next to one of the clothes shops, in the first of a terrace of two-storey stone buildings.

Painted white cornices and stone columns surrounded the glass shop front. The window display was made up of a tray of gold rings, several intricate bracelets displayed on short plinths, and exquisite necklaces hanging on bust-shaped boards.

And beside them, there was a smiling poster of Tasha, wearing a gold necklace with a diamond teardrop and matching earrings.

Keya was overcome by a sudden dizziness, and she leaned against the shop window and closed her eyes.

"Are you all right?" demanded a haughty female voice.

Keya opened her eyes and pushed her head off the shop window. "Yes, I think so. It was just the shock of seeing Tasha's photo."

The face of the formally-suited woman, in her late 60s, softened and she asked, "Were you a friend of hers?"

"Not exactly, although we did meet a couple of times last week." Keya straightened the blue blazer she was wearing as she composed herself. "I'm actually a police officer on Miss Nkosi's case. I need to speak to Ezra, Mr Farmer. Is he working today?"

"Personally, I don't think he should be, but he said he couldn't bear to be by himself at home. He's in the office upstairs. Come into the shop and I'll tell him you're here. You are?" the woman asked as she held the white shop door open for Keya.

"Sergeant Keya Varma."

Keya sat down on a leather chair and waited while the shop assistant spoke on a phone. When she finished, she called across to Keya, "He'll be with you in a minute. Would you like a tea or coffee?"

"Coffee, please," replied Keya.

"What sort? Latte, cappuccino ..."

"Cappuccino, please."

The woman disappeared.

Several minutes later, the bell above the entrance jangled, and the door opened. Keya looked up as an excited young couple entered the shop.

The shop assistant reappeared carrying a piece of black slate with Keya's coffee and two round shortbread biscuits on it.

How cute, Keya thought, but also smart. Was there something similar she could do for her cafe? And should she have sample biscuits to give away, to encourage customers to buy more, or would it stop them ordering any at all?

"I'll be with you in a minute," the shop assistant said to the young couple. Her voice was friendly and welcoming. Keya considered that she must be very good at her job, with the experience of distinguishing genuine shoppers from those who were merely browsing.

"I'm sure Mr Farmer won't be much longer," said the shop assistant as she placed the slate on a white table beside Keya's chair.

"Thank you," Keya said.

The shop assistant smiled before turning and approaching the young couple. "Good morning. I see you're looking at our display of rings. Is this a special occasion?"

"Hello, Keya." So intently had Keya been watching the young couple that she hadn't seen or heard Ezra arrive. He looked pale and drawn, with large black bags under his eyes.

"I presume you've come to question me about Tasha and how she died," he said, his voice flat and unemotional.

"I'm afraid so, although the cause of death is still unknown."

Ezra manoeuvred the chair next to Keya and sat down so they were at right angles to each other.

"First, the worry and anxiety when she went missing. That was bad enough, but now she's dead." He closed his eyes and massaged his forehead. "It's a never-ending nightmare."

In an empathetic voice, Keya said, "And now you have to answer my questions. I'll try to be as brief as possible, but we do need to know more about Tasha's background, your relationship with her, when you last saw her. We also need to know your movement between midnight on Thursday and eight am on Friday morning."

Erza's eyes widened, and he stared incredulously at her. "You want my alibi?"

The shop assistant glanced across at him before returning to her customers. She removed a tray of gold rings from a glass cabinet.

"We have to ask all those close to her, until we are certain of the cause of death."

"Well, as I told you before. Tasha and I had supper with my parents at The Falcon in Cirencester on Thursday evening. Tasha was distant and only picked at her food. I know she resented my parents organising our wedding."

"Resented is a strong word," Keya observed.

Ezra drew his lips together before clarifying, "OK, let's just say she was overwhelmed."

"Had she spoken to you about eloping and leaving all the formal wedding celebrations behind?"

"I think you know she had. But my parents. They've been so generous and they're paying for everything. I couldn't let them down and just take off with Tasha."

It was Keya's turn to purse her lips.

"Look, we only had a week to go and then it would all be over."

Keya refrained from adding that perhaps it was one week too many. "So, you drove Tasha back to her cottage. Why didn't you stay with her?"

A flush spread across Ezra's cheeks. "Our parents asked us not to spend the night at each other's places. Not until after we were married."

Keya waited for Ezra to expand.

"I think they thought it looked better. You know how people gossip round here."

Keya did. But would they be concerned that a couple about to get married spent the night together? Surely, most people in the Cotswolds would consider it normal behaviour these days.

"As you left Rose Cottage, you said you saw a large saloon car parked beside the green and the occupant turned the headlights off as you approached."

"Yes."

"And have you remembered any more about the car or its occupant, or anything else about the village that night?"

"Nothing that stands out. I was tired and just wanted to get home."

"And tell me your movements on Friday morning?"

"Much the same as any other day when I'm working from home. I woke just after seven and started work. I tried to call Tasha about ten to eight but when she didn't reply I presumed she was still asleep. I went for a run and then showered and changed. I was working when you phoned me looking for Tasha."

"Can anyone vouch for you?"

"No, I live alone, and I didn't see anyone on the tracks through the wood where I run."

So if Ezra needed an alibi, he didn't have one.

Keya thought of other questions she should ask while she was here. "We don't know much about Tasha's life in London. Is there anyone from there, or her past, who might have wanted to harm her? The modelling industry is notoriously cut-throat."

"She was only on the margins of it, and her marketing job helped her stay grounded, as did her sweet nature. She was never pushy. That's one reason my parents chose her for the face of Farmers Jewellery."

Ezra glanced towards the young couple as the shop assistant asked, "And when's the big day?"

He winced, and the pain etched across his face was clear to see.

"One last question," said Keya. "The gold heart and necklace you gave Tasha. Any reason she might have taken it off?"

"Taken it off? No! She loved that necklace. Said it helped her keep strong, even when she was feeling like it was all too much. Where did you find it?"

"On a bench, beside the river."

"The river she was found in?"

"Yes," Keya replied simply.

The colour drained from Ezra's face. "Sorry, I can't deal with this. Not now."

He jumped up, bumping into the young couple, before disappearing upstairs.

"I'm so sorry," apologised the shop assistant. "Would you like a matching pair of earrings or a bracelet to go with your engagement ring?"

"I like the necklace the model in your window is wearing. Although she's beautiful and I don't think it will look the same on me."

The shop assistant looked at the young woman and said, "We are all beautiful in our own way. Don't you forget that."

CHAPTER THIRTY-SIX

Peggy was waiting by Keya's VW Polo when she returned to Cheltenham Hospital.

"How did it go?" asked Keya.

"Better than expected," Peggy replied, matter-of-factly. "I've got some new medication and they said they'd keep an eye on me for a few months before deciding if surgery is necessary. So that's good news."

Her tone was forcefully positive as she said, "And at least I've lived a full life, unlike that poor girl, Natasha Nkosi. Do they know what happened to her?"

Keya shook her head.

Peggy's hand shot to her mouth. After a moment, she cried, "Are you investigating her death? Have I kept you away from it? I'm so sorry."

"Don't be," insisted Keya. "I am part of the investigating team, but don't worry, I've been working on her case while you had your appointment."

Peggy leaned towards Keya and lowered her voice. "Really. Have you been questioning a suspect?"

"Peggy," Keya remonstrated. "You know I can't talk about it."

"No, of course not." Peggy, suitably chastised, climbed into Keya's car. As Keya turned on the engine Peggy said, "Drop me in Cirencester. I need to do some shopping and then I can catch the bus home."

"Are you sure?" asked Keya.

"Certain." Peggy clicked her seatbelt in place and was silent for the rest of the journey.

When Keya entered Inspector Evan's team room at Cirencester Police Station, she was greeted by Ryan who asked, "Do you know a Detective Otto?"

Keya groaned. "He's not a police officer. That's his social media persona. Why?"

"He called for you today but I spoke to him and we had a useful chat. He said you asked him to look into Natasha's life in London and he's put together a folder of photos he found online. Isn't it amazing what people post and the information freely available if only we had time to look for it?"

"Which usually we don't, so a big thank you to this particular member of the public. Did he find anything useful about the case?"

"Actually, he did. He sent me a link to his file, and I think you'll want to look at these."

Keya moved round Ryan's desk and, standing next to him, stared at his monitor.

Leaning closer she exclaimed, "That's Dan, my fit-out contractor. He implied that he and Tasha only met up again when she moved to the Cotswolds. But he was lying, again."

"It seems so," Ryan agreed.

"Where is Dan?"

"He's still down in the holding cells. According to Stan, Chief Inspector Greg gave authority for Inspector Evans to hold him overnight."

Keya glanced up at Inspector Evans' door and asked, "Where is he?"

"Stan says he's been called to headquarters in Gloucester."

"Has there been a breakthrough in the case?"

"No, which I think is why he's been called in. The papers are pressing for information about how Natasha died."

"At least we can pass that one to SOCO. Why don't you and I interview Dan again. I should think he's fed up of being in his cell."

The duty sergeant brought Dan to the same interview room they'd used the previous day.

With the formalities completed, Dan asked, "How long are you going to keep me here? Do you really think I hurt Tasha? I've told you. She was just a friend. But one I was concerned about."

Keya leaned back in her chair and studied Dan. "But was she just a friend? And have you been telling us the complete truth?"

Dan glanced from Keya to Ryan and back again.

Keya noticed him clench his hands into fists on top of the table, although he quickly relaxed them.

"Social media causes the police lots of problems, but it can also be incredibly helpful. Like these photos which were posted on it."

Keya turned over a blown-up photo Ryan had printed off, which she'd kept face down on the interview table. She pushed it toward Dan and turned over a second photo.

Dan looked at the photos and gulped. "I can explain."

"Good, go ahead," invited Keya.

"Tasha and I met by chance in a bar. I'd been at an awards ceremony in London, and she'd just finished a shoot for a major fashion house. It was a trendy bar and I bumped into another friend from college. He was older than Tasha and me, but he'd done well for himself and was an assistant editor on a national magazine.

"He, Tasha and I started talking. Tasha invited us to join her and her friends at a party and, as David, my friend, knew most of the people there he slotted straight in. And he proudly paraded Tasha about. I think those photos were taken towards the end of the evening, well my evening anyway. The others went off clubbing, but I had to get up early for work, so I left them around midnight."

"Were you jealous?" Ryan asked.

"I ..." Dan hesitated, and then sighed. "Yes, but how could I compete? With David or any of the group. They all had glamorous jobs in London. I'm merely a shopfitter from the Cotswolds. Besides, she was already engaged."

Keya glanced at Ryan and asked, "When were these photos taken?"

"Let me go and check," said Ryan pushing back his chair.

"No need," said Dan flatly. "Just under five months ago. I left the company I was working for a week after that and set up on my own."

Keya's brain ticked. It was unlikely but, "Did anything happen between David and Tasha?"

Dan clasped his hands together and looked down at the table. He muttered, "I didn't realise anything had. Not until Tasha told me in the early hours of Friday morning. I felt dreadful. I introduced them and David took advantage of her. He might have been the father of her child."

"Were you angry with Tasha for choosing David over you?" asked Keya.

"No, of course not. Why should I be?"

"Because you keep lying to us."

"To protect Tasha," Dan protested.

"Are you sure it's not to protect yourself?"

Keya leaned forward and said, "The inspector, and others in the case, already distrust you. That's why you spent the night in the cells. So if we discover that someone else was involved in Tasha's death, you're the first person we'll be looking at. And you were the last person to see her alive."

CHAPTER THIRTY-SEVEN

Keya asked the duty sergeant to return Dan to the holding cells. They couldn't keep him much longer without formally arresting him, but at the moment there was no crime to charge him with.

Keya believed Dan genuinely cared for Tasha and wanted to help her, but had he become jealous and turned his love against her? Had she rejected him and accepted others who, in Dan's eyes, were less worthy than himself?

Keya didn't know the answers.

But there was one other person who might be able to provide some answers, and that was Tasha's brother, Nate. She needed to speak to him.

Keya called Inspector Sue and asked, "How is the family this morning?"

"Barely holding it together. Thankfully Naomi is here, but I'm worried about Solomon. I can't persuade him to eat anything and he looks dreadful. Linda's barely speaking to him, and Nate keeps disappearing. Tasha's death is driving this family apart."

"It's an incredibly stressful time for them all. Is Nate there at the moment?" asked Keya.

"Yes, do you want to speak to him?"

"I do. Can you make sure he doesn't disappear again? I think I'll leave Ryan at the station to follow up leads, so would you mind sitting in with me while I question Nate?"

"Not at all. It'll be good to actually do something. The waiting around on this case has been draining."

"I'll be with you in half an hour."

Keya finished her call and Ryan asked, "What leads would you like me to follow up?"

"Anything else you can find out about Tasha's life in London over the past six months? And can you look into the David character Dan told us about?"

"Sure, and good luck with Nate."

"Thanks," said Keya as she left the team room.

Keya arrived at The Manor House Hotel at half past twelve. Inspector Sue had sent a message that she and Nate were in the function room, so Keya walked along the corridor from hotel reception and knocked on the closed brown door.

"Come in," called Sue.

Keya entered and saw Sue and Nate eating sandwiches and chatting amiably. Good, Nate appeared relaxed and, even better, there looked to be enough food for her.

"Busy morning?" asked Sue.

"Yes, I suppose it has been." Keya sat down and poured herself a glass of water from the jug on the table. She didn't want to expand on her day's interviews with Nate present.

Inspector Sue pushed a clingfilm covered plate towards her. "These are vegetarian."

Keya smiled gratefully at her. "Thank you. So often in the middle of an investigation, I don't find time to eat."

"I know. I have to look after Chief Inspector Greg, or he'd fall over from fatigue and lack of food."

"These sandwiches aren't bad," said Nate, leaning back in his chair and taking a bite out of half a brown roll filled with what looked like chicken.

Keya ignored the sandwiches for the moment and opened her notebook. "Nate, we're trying to establish what happened to your sister while we wait for the results of the post-mortem."

"What can I tell you?" Nate asked.

"Why were you arguing with her the afternoon before she disappeared?"

Nate choked and coughed. He leaned forward and grabbed a can of Diet Coke resting on the table and took a glug. When he recovered, he said, "What do you mean?"

"A witness saw you enter Rose Cottage on Thursday afternoon. She heard raised voices and said you stormed out. It isn't unusual for brothers and sisters to disagree and argue. I just wondered what your row was about."

Nate shuffled in his seat and replied, "It wasn't really an argument. I was just trying to persuade Tasha to go ahead with her wedding. That in just over a week it would be all over and if she then wanted to hide away in the Cotswolds, away from life, away from London, that was her prerogative. But everyone was looking forward to her wedding. It would be a fantastic party."

"But Tasha didn't want the party, did she? Or the big wedding with all the guests her future in-laws wanted to impress?"

"I'm sure once she was there, she'd love it. What bride doesn't revel in the attention?"

"One who's anxious," replied Keya, suddenly realising she'd spoken her thoughts out loud.

Nate waved his hand dismissively. "Every bride is nervous. Marriage is a big step."

This time, Keya made sure she kept her thoughts to herself. Nate had never been married, and he was hardly qualified to speak on behalf of all brides.

"So that was the only reason you and Tasha raised your voices? Because you were trying to persuade her to go through with her wedding."

"Yeah, that's right."

"And how does Tasha's death affect you personally?"

"I'm devastated, of course. Losing my sister." Nate's voice was smooth and measured, but his eyes darted to the door and there was a wariness about him.

Keya knew there was something more. Something he was hiding. Naomi had hinted at it.

"But financially? Tasha not getting married must have hit you?"

Nate flinched and his voice sounded strained as he answered, "I don't know what you mean."

Keya decided to stop dancing around the subject. She leaned forward and asked, "How did you gain financially from Tasha's marriage?"

"I didn't," he squeaked.

Keya tilted her head to one side and raised her eyebrows. She didn't say anything as she watched Nate squirm.

Nate looked at Inspector Sue as if she would help him out, but her face remained impassive.

"It wasn't much," blurted Nate.

Keya waited for him to continue.

"Just a few thousand pounds Ezra's family agreed to invest in my new business. But they'll get their money back tenfold. Battery recycling is the next big thing."

"Of course it is," agreed Keya, her voice unemotional. "And how many thousands were the Farmers investing?"

"Twelve," Nate replied in a small voice.

Keya leaned back. Up to now her impression of Ezra's parents, who she hadn't met, was that they were controlling and set on organising a large, elaborate wedding to impress their friends and local bigwigs. But was that true?

They'd agreed to pay Solomon enough for Linda's hip operation, and Nate £12,000 for his business, which Keya had no doubt was not the next big thing.

The Farmers must really have wanted Tasha to marry their son. But because of his happiness, or because they'd have the face of Farmers Jewellery in the family?

Perhaps they thought they wouldn't have to pay Tasha for her modelling work, and they could use her to impress their friends and potential clients.

Keya scratched her cheek. It appeared nobody's motives in this case were simple or based solely on Tasha's and Ezra's future happiness.

"How was Tasha when you left her on Thursday?" asked Keya.

"Upset, but she was emotional. All brides are before their weddings."

Keya snapped. "No, they're not. And as you are not, and never will be, a bride, stop answering for them."

Inspector Sue placed her hand on the table and, in a soothing voice, said, "I think what Sergeant Varma is trying to say is that all brides have different experiences, and we shouldn't generalise."

"Exactly," agreed Keya, still annoyed with Nate, and herself. She peeled back the clingfilm and removed a sandwich from her plate. She bit into it and wrinkled her nose. It was nothing she'd ever tasted before. The filling was a paste which definitely contained tomato, and egg, and a hint of cheese?

"You're right," admitted Nate. "Tasha was upset when I left, and it was selfish of me to storm out and leave her like that. But I was so annoyed. She had no idea how much her wedding meant to me."

"£12,000," muttered Keya, between bites.

"I'm sure you intended to go back and smooth things over with your sister," Inspector Sue suggested, trying to calm things down.

"Oh yes, I did. I visited Ezra, and he told me not to worry. Tasha had agreed to go ahead with the wedding. So I drove to Coln Akeman, and that's when I met you." He looked at Keya.

She squinted. "You met Ezra on Friday morning?"

"Yes, we went for a walk and a talk."

Why had Ezra not mentioned that? And why was this investigation going round in circles?

Keya finished her sandwich and said, "To recap. You drove down from London with your parents on Thursday. In the afternoon you visited Tasha to make sure she'd go through with her wedding so you'd get the investment you needed for your business venture. You both argued and you left. And that was the last time you saw your sister?"

Nate stared blankly back at her. Then he covered his mouth with his hand and let out a low moan.

Keya pressed on. "Where were you between midnight on Thursday and eight am on Friday?"

"Here, in bed," replied Nate in a small voice. "I just managed to wake up in time for breakfast, which finishes at nine."

The hotel could vouch for his appearance at breakfast, although he could have driven to Coln Akeman and back before he sat down to eat.

"Can I go now?" asked Nate, his voice flat and unemotional.

"Yes," replied Inspector Sue. "That's enough questions for today."

And as Nate shuffled from the room, Keya knew she was right.

"Thank you," said Keya to Inspector Sue. "I shouldn't have let him rattle me."

"It's not easy interviewing people, especially when you know the victim, as you did. But it's easy for us to sit back and judge other people's actions with the benefit of hindsight, and a more rounded picture. Nate is not someone who thinks far beyond his own view of the world."

"You're right. About all of it. And it's interesting he mentions visiting Ezra. Ezra omitted to tell me about that when I spoke to him this morning." Keya picked up and munched another sandwich. When she finished, she said, "These are great. What's the filling?"

"It has a very strange name. Mock crab, although it doesn't resemble crab in the least. Apparently, it's an old war time recipe used when there was rationing."

"How interesting. I'll have to look it up. I'm opening a cafe you see, or I will be if we stop finding dead bodies at the site and I don't arrest the fit-out contractor for murder." Keya shook her head. "I hope SOCO provides the results of the post-mortem soon, so we know if anyone else was involved."

Inspector Sue nodded. "But whatever they say, I can't help thinking that this was an unnecessary death. That if only someone had listened and tried to help Natasha, we wouldn't be where we are today."

A light flashed outside the window.

"What was that?" asked Keya.

Inspector Sue's motherly face clouded over. "I'll kill that digital detective." And she stormed from the room.

Keya looked out of the window and saw a young man holding a phone up against the glass. Was nowhere private or secure?

CHAPTER THIRTY-EIGHT

Keya felt despondent as she walked into her team room at Cirencester Police Station.

Ryan stopped tapping away on his keyboard and asked, "What's up?"

"People," replied Keya. "Why are they so selfish?"

Ryan didn't respond but stared at Keya, so she continued, "First, we have Tasha's family, some of whom acted in self-interest and looked at Tasha's marriage as a way to benefit personally. And then, while some members of the public have been very helpful and provided us with information, others are using Tasha's tragedy to boost their own online profile, or achieve fame or notoriety."

"That's too true," agreed Ryan. "I've just been speaking to Inspector Evans and Chief Inspector Greg about the online reports, accusations, and theories surrounding Tasha's death. There are even several cases of doxing."

"What on earth's that?" cried Keya.

"It's when someone deliberately posts someone else's personal information online. Chief Inspector Greg's unit is trying to track down several people who've posted photos of Tasha partying and who've implied she was taking drugs, drinking too much and, well, being promiscuous, although that's not the term they've used."

"But that's not fair. It makes Tasha out to be ..." Keya didn't bother to finish the sentence but flopped down onto her seat behind her desk.

"The trouble is, we can't do anything about it," admitted Ryan. "Doxing isn't illegal, however much it upsets an individual or, in this case, a family."

"Well, I'm not sure how much notice this family will take of others at the moment, as they have their own conduct to consider. But if Solomon sees it ... You better call Inspector Sue and tell her. I need a walk."

Clouds were beginning to form as Keya walked around the streets of Cirencester. Cafe owners were removing or stacking up outdoor tables and chairs and shoppers hurried, as if aware their time was limited.

The rain started falling when she was still three minutes away from the station and by the time she pushed open the door into reception, her blazer was soaking. As was her hair. But at least her mind felt clearer.

Back in the team room, she found Ryan had been joined by Inspector Evans and Chief Inspector Greg.

"Ah, here she is," announced the inspector.

"Sorry, I needed some fresh air," Keya apologised, removing her blazer and hanging it across two pegs, hoping it would dry before she went out again.

"We have the results from SOCO," said Chief Inspector Greg, and without further preamble announced, "Natasha Nkosi drowned. And there is no evidence that anyone else was involved."

"So what are you saying? She did it herself?" Keya leaned against Nick's desk, feeling despondent.

"She might have committed suicide, or her death might have been an accident. She could have been out walking and slipped or, if it was dark, missed her footing and fallen in the river. I'm not sure we'll ever know. But it'll be up to the coroner to make the final verdict."

Inspector Evans asked, "Have you found anything in the course of your enquiries to support one conclusion or another?"

Keya shook her head. "Her father and her brother both gained financially from her wedding. And her mother would have received a new hip, but she didn't know that. And Daniel Hirst, who I presume we are still holding, didn't gain at all. In fact, he lost the chance of a relationship with Tasha."

"So we have to turn to her state of mind," said the chief inspector.

"She doesn't appear to have visited any doctors, but I think everyone close to her will now admit she was anxious and depressed. Because of the baby she lost, and the stress of her 'wedding of the year'. But to take her own life? I don't know." Keya sighed.

Ryan, who had returned to tapping on his computer, suddenly exclaimed, "Of course!"

"Of course what, Constable?" demanded Inspector Evans.

"That explains it."

"Explains what?" Inspector Evans sounded annoyed.

Ryan stood and lifted his computer monitor and turned it to face into the room. Placing it back on his desk he insisted, "Look at this picture of the Weeping Widow ghost. Does it remind you of anyone?"

"Remind me?" replied the inspector in a confused tone.

"Natasha Nkosi," stated Chief Inspector Greg.

Keya jumped up and, pushing Inspector Evans out of the way, stared at Ryan's monitor. "Mrs Angles' shawl. She said she'd lent it to Tasha, but I didn't believe her. But that's what Tasha is wearing over her white pyjama bottoms. Tasha was the ghost!"

"And that's why there haven't been any sightings since she disappeared," reasoned Ryan.

"Good work, Constable." Which was rare praise from Inspector Evans.

"So what now?" asked Keya.

"The family needs to be told about the post-mortem," replied the inspector. "I suggest you and the Chief Inspector arrange to meet them at The Manor House Hotel. I understand Sue has the use of a room which will serve your purpose. Take Daniel Hirst with you. Constable, can you tell the duty sergeant to release him without charge and bring him up here? Sergeant, contact Mr Farmer and ask him to meet you at the hotel."

Chief Inspector Greg added, "And I'll call Sue and ask her to gather the family members together and make sure Nate doesn't do another disappearing act."

So the Chief Inspector had been receiving updates from Inspector Sue, thought Keya.

Chief Inspector Greg and Inspector Evans entered the inspector's office and closed the door as Ryan left the team room.

Relieved to have the room to herself, Keya sat down at her desk, picked up her office phone, and called Ezra.

"Sergeant Varma, any news?"

"We're expecting some shortly," she lied. She knew that if he pressed, she'd probably blurt out the results of the post-mortem and she didn't want to do that over the phone.

"We'd like to tell you and Tasha's family at the same time, so can you meet me at The Manor House Hotel in Coln St Aldwyns?"

"When?"

"As soon as you can get there."

Sounding suddenly energised, Ezra declared, "I'm leaving right now."

Keya finished the call. It would take Ezra at least half an hour, more like forty-five minutes to reach the hotel. She should be able to make it back there in twenty minutes.

Ryan returned to the team room, escorting Dan.

Keya motioned for him to sit next to her in Nick's office chair.

Dan looked haunted, and she noticed the stubble stippling his face. He was still wearing yesterday's creased clothes. She knew she was supposed to take him with her and break the news of the post-mortem to all those involved at the same time, but was it fair to impose Dan on the family at this difficult time?

And for Dan, was it appropriate or reasonable to expect him to confront Tasha's family in this state?

"Dan, I'm sorry for keeping you here, but we now have the results of the post-mortem. We haven't told Tasha's immediate family yet, so please keep this to yourself."

"I will. I'm going straight home for a shower, but please, tell me how Tasha died. I've been tormenting myself sitting in that cell."

"I'm afraid we don't know exactly how it happened, but the cause of death is drowning."

"She fell in the river?"

"That's certainly one possible answer."

Dan sat back. "Another is that she deliberately jumped in, or someone pushed her."

"It will be for the coroner to decide, although there is currently no evidence that anyone else was involved."

"Poor Tasha. What led her to do that?"

"I think you know."

Dan bowed his head. "I do. If only I'd done more to help her."

CHAPTER THIRTY-NINE

Inspector Sue met Keya and Chief Inspector Greg in the reception of The Manor House Hotel.

"Everyone's here," she said. "Ezra Farmer arrived a few minutes ago."

"Good," nodded the Chief Inspector. "Lead the way."

Inside the hotel's function room, a second table had been pushed against the first and more metal chairs arranged around them both. Most of them were occupied by Tasha's family. Linda sat next to her husband, cradling his hand in hers. Solomon was slumped in his seat and his face was vacant. Naomi and Nate glanced unpleasantly at each other, and Ezra stopped his pacing when Keya entered.

"Please take a seat," Inspector Sue indicated to a spare chair for Ezra and sat down next to him. Keya and the chief inspector remained standing. Keya's hair and jacket still felt damp, but she ignored them. This was important.

Chief Inspector Greg breathed in and considered each of those sitting at the table in turn. Finally, he said, "This case has been very personal to me, and I hope you'll appreciate, in time, that myself and my team did everything we could to find a satisfactory outcome. But that wasn't to be. Natasha died on the morning she disappeared."

Linda gasped, but Solomon only grimaced, possibly because Linda had squeezed his hand too tightly.

"She entered the River Coln and drowned," continued the chief inspector.

Ezra nodded and muttered, "So it was drowning."

Naomi asked in a small voice, "Did she kill herself?"

"We don't know," replied the chief inspector. "The coroner will make the formal pronouncement, but the police will not be pursing this any further. There is no evidence that anyone else was involved."

Around the table there was an audible sigh and Ezra, Nate and Linda all looked relieved.

"But she could have killed herself?" pressed Naomi.

"Her death may have been accidental, and she fell in, or she could have jumped, we don't know."

"And my necklace?" asked Ezra.

"We've no idea why she took it off."

"Have you found a note?" asked Nate.

"No, but seventy to seventy-five per cent of people who take their own lives, don't leave a letter stating why they did it," explained Chief Inspector Greg.

"I'm not sure I could write one," muttered Naomi.

"Unfortunately, this will fuel more speculation in the press and social media about Natasha, the life she led, you, her family, her upcoming wedding and, of course, her mental state. News about her pregnancy may leak and other untruths may be circulated. It will be a difficult time for you all." Chief Inspector Greg nodded at Inspector Sue.

Inspector Sue reassured the family. "I shall remain your police contact. And if you don't want to talk to the press, I'm happy to help write statements which the chief inspector and his team will distribute. There is no need for you to speak to anyone else."

"But the press won't give up," cried Naomi. "Someone follows me every time I leave the hotel for a walk or run."

"I'm afraid there isn't anything else we can do, apart from reiterating with them that you should all be left alone to deal with this tragic event." Chief Inspector Greg looked at Keya.

Her eyes widened. What did he expect her to do?

He mouthed, "The ghost."

"Oh, yes." Keya looked around the family group. "Some of you may know that there was a lot of excitement in Coln Akeman after several appearances of a ghost, which was given the name the Weeping Widow. There was no reason for this except the ghostly figure resembled a woman. My colleague has searched the internet and found footage and photographs of the so-called ghost and we now think it was actually Tasha, out walking late at night."

"You're joking!" cried Nate.

"We're happy to share our information with you, but it may be no coincidence that the ghost hasn't been sighted since Tasha disappeared."

"And I thought ghosts were supposed to appear after your death, not before." Naomi slowly shook her head.

Keya shivered violently. Had Tasha just walked across her grave? And would she torment her dreams, asking why she hadn't helped her? That poor, lonely young woman.

"At least we're all in the clear," declared Nate, jumping up.

Keya stared at him. She took a step forward and said, "Tasha is dead." She paused and looked round the table. "And every single one of you is responsible for that. Because of what you did," she ignored Solomon but stared at Nate, who stepped back, "or didn't do." This time, her eyes fell on Naomi.

"You knew the fragile state she was in, Linda, but you refused to help. You put your husband's wishes in front of your daughter's needs. Who could she turn to if not her mother? And you, Naomi. Why didn't you come down and visit her? Is your work so important, or inflexible, that you couldn't spend time with your sister?"

"I didn't know," sobbed Naomi.

"And you, Nate, and your father. Tasha's wedding was something you were profiting from. So it had to go ahead. Neither of you listened to her. You just pushed her further into it."

Finally, Keya turned to Ezra. Her voice softened slightly as she said, "I know you loved her, and she loved you back. But would you have listened to her any more after the wedding than before? You put the needs, the demands of your parents, before your bride, and for that, Tasha paid the ultimate price."

Keya stepped back, surveying those at the table. "She is no longer with us, but each and every one of you has to live with the guilt. With the knowledge that you could have prevented her death. I just hope you learn from this and that you live better lives and help others as you should have helped Tasha."

Exhausted and exasperated, Keya fled the room.

She walked out of the front door. The recent rainfall had cleared the air, and she gulped in deep lungfuls of fresh, pure air. Oxygen, the essence of life.

CHAPTER FORTY

Chief Inspector Greg stepped out of The Manor House Hotel's front door and said, "That was quite a statement."

"Should I go back and apologise?" Keya asked.

"No, I've left Sue with the family. They're all stunned, but perhaps highlighting their failings will help them address their guilt now, rather than allowing it to fester. I'm not sure Solomon took it in, but perhaps he's already paid the price for his action. He's a broken man. Hopefully, as you said, the younger ones can live a better, more meaningful life and help others."

A bee buzzed round them.

"And you were right not to bring Dan. Although your inspector thought that if anyone had killed her, it was him, he actually did the most to help her. As did you and your sister. I hope that neither of you will beat yourselves up. There really is nothing more you could have done."

Keya spotted the bee and watched as it landed on a purple flower.

"I'll go back and answer any questions the family has, and then drive you back to the station."

As Chief Inspector Greg turned and left Keya, something flashed near the hotel gateway. A camera lens? Keya walk round the side of the hotel to a small seating area. Two elderly ladies were sipping cups of tea, the floral decorated teapot sitting on the table between them.

Keya sat down and for several minutes just let herself be.

Her phone vibrating in her trouser pocket disturbed her reverie.

"Sis, what's up?" she asked, answering the call.

"Where are you?" countered Zivah.

"Coln St Aldwyns."

Zivah whispered to someone else, and then said, "Can you meet us at The Axeman in twenty minutes?"

Keya had no idea of the time. "I don't have my car," she said.

"Can someone drop you off and I'll drive you home later?"

Keya suddenly realised how excited her sister sounded. And she rarely called and asked her to meet for a drink or meal. This must be important.

"Of course. I'm sure the chief inspector can drop me there."

"Great. See you in twenty."

Keya checked her watch. Half past five. Standing up, she wandered round to the front of the hotel where Chief Inspector Greg was standing, looking round.

"There you are. Sue's staying with the family, but I need to get home, and drop you off on my way."

"Do you mind taking me to the pub in Coln Akeman instead, to meet my sister?"

"Not at all. In fact, that's much easier than going into Cirencester."

Chief Inspector Greg drove the short distance to Coln Akeman.

"Thank you," said Keya as she climbed out of his car.

"Thank you for all your hard work," replied the chief inspector. "And I look forward to working with you again soon."

Keya closed the car door as the chief inspector grinned at her, but said no more.

What was that about? she wondered.

"Keya," shouted Gilly.

Keya turned round and saw Gilly and Dr Peter sitting at a table outside The Axeman.

"We've sneaked out for half an hour while the kids finish their homework," explained Gilly. "And what brings you here? Not more police work, I hope."

Keya pulled out a chair and slumped onto it. "No, I can't deal with any more today."

"You need a stiff drink," said Dr Peter.

"You know I don't drink," replied Keya.

"Then perhaps a coffee to perk you up." Dr Peter disappeared inside the pub.

"You know that man who was loitering around the garden at the weekend?" Gilly said.

"Otto?"

"That's the one. Well, he knocked on our door earlier with a bottle of wine and an apology for trying to climb into our garden. And then Peter and him got talking, and it transpires he's a computer expert. He's taking a look at the surgery system next week."

"That's good," replied Keya, dozily.

"Here you are." Dr Peter placed a cappuccino on the table in front of her.

Keya sipped the foamy liquid. She didn't usually drink coffee this late in the day, but it tasted good.

"We received the results of Tasha Nkosi's post-mortem this afternoon."

Keya unburdened herself on Gilly and Dr Peter, who listened attentively and only asked a few clarifying questions.

Aadi and Zivah joined them as Keya explained her visit to the family and Ezra at The Manor House Hotel to tell them the results of the post-mortem.

"You didn't?" Zivah exclaimed, when Keya told them about her outburst.

"But do you feel better for it?" asked Dr Peter.

"I do," Keya admitted, "and as Chief Inspector Greg said, hopefully they will too. It's the sort of tragedy that can fester away and destroy a family. Hopefully they'll deal with their trauma together and come out the stronger for it."

"Well done, Keya. That was very bold of you," said Dr Peter.

"And talking of stronger. The hospital released Uncle Cliff back to the nursing home today. Aunt Beanie says he's rather chipper despite his illness, and is looking forward to sitting on his patio chatting to his friend Edith."

"That's great," Keya acknowledged.

"And now we must go home," Gilly declared, standing up. "Thank you for updating us about the case."

As they left, Zivah asked, "Can we go inside? I'm getting cold sitting out here."

Keya realised she was shivering, and her blazer was still damp.

Aadi insisted they order food before he allowed Zivah to speak, even though she was clearly bursting to tell Keya her news.

Finally Zivah blurted, "We've set a new date. Thursday 27th July. And as it's a weekday, we can use Charbury Castle Hotel."

"That's wonderful," cried Keya.

"But Zivah doesn't want to," said Aadi.

"Get married?"

"No, silly." Zivah gently smacked Keya's arm. "Use the hotel. Not after they cancelled, and then what happened to Tasha. I hope you don't mind, but I contacted Jay, and he said we can still use Windrush Hall. So Aadi and I have spoken to marquee companies, and we have several quotes, and we met a caterer just now in Cirencester who had the most wonderful idea for food which will satisfy the older Indian relatives, but also give a fresh, unique feeling, just as we want for our wedding," gushed Zivah.

Keya smiled. "That's great. But can you still hire the horse?"

"I hope so," giggled Zivah. "I'd forgotten about him."

Zivah's effervescence was just the tonic Keya needed after her day investigating and concluding Tasha's case. Hopefully her sister and Aadi could live an open and honest life together, their way, rather than in a way dictated by their Indian families.

After an enjoyable meal and entertaining stories from Zivah, they finally left the pub. It was dark outside and as Keya glanced across the village green, a ghostly figure stopped, waved and disappeared. She shook her head.

"What is it?" asked Zivah.

Keya smiled. "A spirit laid to rest."

CHAPTER FORTY-ONE

Zivah hugged Keya and whispered, "Don't worry, sis. Everything will be fine."

"Are we ready?" called Gilly Wimsey, from the closed door of the Waterwheel Cafe which led into the antiques centre.

Keya nodded.

"We are," called Zivah.

Keya watched Gilly open the door and thought of the past three weeks.

Since the conclusion of Tasha Nkosi's case, she'd only spent a few days in the office, for team meetings and to brief Ryan who, in her absence, had taken over part of her Rural Engagement Officer role. Luckily, there had been no serious crimes for them to investigate.

She had not been called to testify at Tasha's inquest. That job had fallen to Chief Inspector Greg. Inspector Sue had accompanied him, and she was the one who'd told Keya all about it.

Chief Inspector Greg had given the facts of the case and had mentioned that members of his team were concerned about Tasha's mental state. He'd also raised the issue of the gold chain.

The coroner concluded Tasha had taken the chain off because she'd wanted to consider her forthcoming wedding and her future, but she hadn't meant to leave it on the bench.

Tasha's new doctor had travelled from London for the inquest and testified that there was no history of self-harm in Tasha's medical notes, and she'd not treated Tasha for depression or anxiety.

This was enough for the coroner to rule out suicide and, in the absence of any disease or other illness, he said the only conclusion he could draw was that her death was a tragic accident.

So that was it. Tasha had officially died of accidental drowning. Apparently, it was not uncommon for a person to fall into a river and the shock of the cold water to cause them to gasp, thereby inhaling water which can lead to drowning in a matter of minutes.

Keya wasn't fully convinced by the decision, but she thought it the right one for all involved. Even though she'd had her outburst, and accused the family of neglecting Tasha's needs, she didn't condone the comments flying around on social media, accusing them of everything from murder to driving Tasha to take her own life.

After the inquest, the family's solicitor had spoken to the press urging them, and members of the public, to cease harassing the family and, now that the coroner had made his verdict, requesting that they cease their distressing speculation.

Keya had not seen or spoken to the family again since her outburst, but she knew they had returned to London, and only Nate and Naomi had returned for the coroner's inquest. Ryan said Solomon had been taken to hospital and Naomi was worried that he wouldn't return home.

The first customers through the door were Aunt Beanie, pushing Uncle Cliff in a wheelchair with a walking stick across his lap, accompanied by Norman and Edith, Uncle Cliff's friend from the nursing home.

Keya remembered Edith from a previous case she and Dotty had investigated and was delighted to see the grey-haired lady wearing her customary yellow trousers and matching jacket. But it was her smile that lit up the room.

"Welcome to the Waterwheel Cafe," Keya greeted.

"This is so exciting. I haven't been out for so long," beamed Edith.

"Anything you need doing?" asked Norman.

"I think we're OK, but I'll let you know if we do. And thank you for all your help over the past few weeks."

As well as bringing across the tables and chairs, which had been stored away after Chief Inspector Greg's team left the auction house, Norman had helped hang pictures Keya had bought in the antiques centre, carry load after load of cafe equipment, and generally undertake any odd jobs which needed doing.

Aunt Beanie, wearing a bright red scarf tied at a jaunty angle on the top of her head and a matching red gypsy style skirt, peered into the curve-fronted chiller display counter which Keya had bought from Dan. Originally meant for the deli, it now stood next to the serving area.

Half of it held containers of sandwich ingredients, such as slices of cheese and meats, mixtures of egg mayonnaise and tuna and sweetcorn, and specialist fillings of mock crab and Keya's mum's cold chicken tikka.

The other half displayed a selection of impressive looking cakes and, on the shelf above them, biscuits and traybakes.

"Thank you for the coffee and walnut cake," Keya said to Aunt Beanie.

"It looks rather good in there, although not up to the standard of that carrot cake."

"Gilly made that," replied Keya.

"I love the miniature marzipan carrots," grinned Aunt Beanie. "And is it cream cheese frosting?"

"I think so," said Keya, as Uncle Cliff banged the flagstone floor with his walking stick.

"I think we better join the others," Aunt Beanie conceded.

She pushed Uncle Cliff towards a table beside one of the large floor-to-ceiling windows, which looked out over the slowly turning waterwheel and the River Coln.

"Oh wow! Isn't this great?" exclaimed Edith, staring out of the window.

Next to enter the cafe were Ozzie and Ryan.

"My article about your cafe opening is my last for the Cirencester Times," said Ozzie wistfully.

"So you did get your job in London?" Keya congratulated her.

"Yes, although it's for a magazine rather than a newspaper. But I negotiated freelance work into my contract, as long as it doesn't compete with the magazine. So I can still follow, investigate, and report on news items which interest me."

"Are you excited?" Keya thought Ozzie would be far more enthusiastic about her move. After all, she'd been looking for a position in London for a while.

"I am, but I've realised over the last week how much I'll miss you all."

"And how expensive London is?" added Ryan.

"That too," Ozzie accepted. "But I'm sure it'll be fun once I'm there." Ozzie turned away, stopped, and turned back to Keya. She asked, "Did you ever find out who tried to sell Natasha's story to the London paper?"

Keya, momentarily sad, frowned and shook her head.

"I did. It was her brother Nate."

"That's terrible," exclaimed Keya. "But not really a surprise." She sighed. "I only hope he'll act more considerately in the future."

"Let's hope so." Ozzie followed Ryan across the room.

"Don't forget to come back to visit. And please give the cafe a positive review," called Keya as Ozzie and Ryan walked out of the side door to sit on the outdoor terrace.

"Someone's ordered a slice of my Victoria sponge," enthused Zivah as she walked around the back of the display counter and lifted the cake onto the back shelf. As she cut a large slice, Keya thought how happy she looked.

After the conclusion of Tasha's case, Zivah had unexpectedly quit her job saying that life was too short, and she realised she wanted to enjoy the lead up to, and preparations for, her forthcoming wedding.

But in truth, she'd spent much of her time with Keya setting up the cafe and in return Keya had taught her to cook some recipes, including the deliciously light looking Victoria sponge with whipped cream and fresh raspberry filling.

"Keya," called her mum, from the kitchen serving hatch.

When her mum had learnt that Zivah was assisting Keya, she'd insisted that Zivah also drive her over to help prepare the cafe. She had taken over the kitchen and Keya only hoped she didn't upset the student who was working with her.

Keya approached the serving hatch and her mum whispered, "Remind me what we serve alongside a sandwich."

"Slice the sandwich or panini in half and stack one half at an angle over the other half. Place a pot of coleslaw and a handful of crisps on the plate, along with the small salad we worked out yesterday."

"Yes, I remember that. Very good." Keya's mum turned back to the kitchen and directed the student to remove a panini from the toaster. Keya had employed two students to work in the cafe during their summer holidays. They lived locally and had assisted Dotty last Christmas in her pop-up cafe.

Dotty. As Keya turned back to the busy cafe, she realised how much she missed her friend. She would have been calm and so helpful on this, the cafe's opening day. And afterwards they could have relaxed and enjoyed a cup of tea together.

Zivah hurried up to her and said, "Your boss is sitting at a table outside and he wants a word. And after that, can you help serve food while I take orders?"

Keya smiled at Zivah for her professional and businesslike manner.

As Keya weaved through the full tables, she greeted stallholders and regular antique centre customers.

Gilly Wimsey had left her position at the door and taken a table next to Aunt Beanie, where she was sitting with Dr Peter. They were accompanied by their children, Thomas and Olivia, whose faces were pressed against the glass, watching the waterwheel.

Keya stopped to allow Marmaduke Carey to pass in front of her. He greeted his sister, Aunt Beanie, before sitting in the spare chair next to Gilly.

It was less frenetic outside, although still busy. She and Gilly hadn't built a permanent structure to shade customers from the sun, but Zivah had bought huge, sail-shaped pieces of colourful fabric which, with Norman's help, they'd hung across the space from tall wooden posts.

Keya found Inspector Evans sitting with Chief Inspector Greg and Inspector Sue.

"You've done a grand job here, lass, well done," said Inspector Evans, nodding his head.

"It looks wonderful," agreed Inspector Sue. "I love these sail shades."

"My sister's idea," Keya admitted.

"I know you're busy, but can you spare us a couple of minutes?" asked the chief inspector, indicating to a spare chair.

Hesitantly, Keya sat down.

"We've sworn Ryan to silence but news in police stations travels fast," began the chef inspector, "which is why I wanted to update you before you come back to work next week. I'm delighted to say that Nick Unwin has been promoted to inspector and will be heading up the media team at headquarters."

"Good riddance," muttered Inspector Evans, and quickly coughed to cover up his indiscretion.

"Which leaves your team short of an officer."

"So I'm joining you," beamed Inspector Sue.

"But …" began Keya.

"I know, you already have an inspector," Sue glanced across at Inspector Evans, "and I said I'd be happy to demote to the role of sergeant …"

"But that would impact her pension," interjected the chief inspector.

"So I'll keep my rank, but Dai is still the boss."

Keya frowned.

Sue laughed. "I mean Inspector Evans. I'm less than two years away from retirement and the missing person team's dynamic will change now."

"Why?" asked Keya, struggling to keep up with the thread of the conversation.

"Because I'm leaving and joining Cirencester Station as the Chief Inspector in Charge," the chief inspector explained.

"Keya," Zivah called from the doorway into the cafe.

Keya stood and clarified, "So you'll be our big boss?"

Chief Inspector Greg grinned and patted his stomach. "I thought I was in good shape."

Keya smiled lopsidedly at him, turned to Sue and said, "And you'll be working with Ryan and me?"

"I'm looking forward to it, Keya," said Sue, "but I think you're needed."

Keya left her police colleagues and the next few hours raced by as she served sandwiches, quiche and salad, and filled baked potatoes.

The cakes and traybakes were also popular, and she was relieved the company she'd hired the coffee machine from had sent a barista to help them and show them how to make different types of coffee.

The lunch crowd left and was replaced by customers ordering tea and cakes.

"This is fabulous," Peggy greeted her. "I told Derek we just had to come and see the result of all your hard work. And it's a good excuse to catch up with Marge." Keya followed Peggy's gaze to her friend from the WI who was already sitting at one of the wooden tables.

At half past five, Zivah finally shut the door and wearily announced, "We're closed."

Keya's mum stood in the kitchen doorway and wiped her hands on her apron. "You'll need me if it's always going to be this busy."

"Thanks, Mum, but I doubt it will be. But I am grateful to all my friends and the local community for their support today, and to all of you for your help."

"Zivah, we need to make more cakes tonight, and be here early in the morning to prepare more sandwich fillings," instructed their mum.

Zivah smiled and turned towards Keya, shrugging her shoulders.

Keya smiled back. Her cafe was now their cafe. Hers, her sister's, and her mum's, and it felt great.

Vanilla Chai and a Vanishing Victim

Will Zivah finally get married? Can Keya juggle her cafe and her police work? What happens when she's compelled to work on another case?

A missing child. A half-baked ransom demand. Can a community cop sift through clues and rescue the tot before teatime?

Claim your copy of Vanilla Chai and a Vanishing Victim on Amazon

Hour is Come

Would you like to read Keya's first case with her friend Dotty? And discover how The Waterwheel Cafe and Dotty Sayers Antique Mystery series began?

Find out and download *Hour is Come,* which is yours to keep when you sign up to my newsletter for updates.

Claim your copy of Hour is Come by visiting VictoriaTait.com

Fake Death

Have you read the first book in the Dotty Sayers Antique Mystery series?

Young widow, Dotty Sayers, is delighted with her new auction house job in Britain's picturesque Cotswolds. But she's shocked by a soldier's death on Remembrance Day. She realises appearances can be deceiving, but can she track down the real culprit and prevent an innocent man from imprisonment?

Claim Your Copy of Fake Death on Amazon

If you enjoyed this book, please tell someone you know. And for those people you don't know, leave a review to help them decide whether or not to read it.

Review on Amazon

For more information visit VictoriaTait.com

UNTITLED